A TEENAGE GIRL FROM A POOR FAMILY IS DAZZLED BY her rich, vivacious friend, but as the friend's behavior grows unstable and dangerous, she must decide whether to cover for her or risk telling the truth to get her the help she needs. A young woman and her mother bask in the envy of their neighbors when the woman receives an offer of marriage from the family of a doctor living in Belgium—though when the offer fails to materialize, that envy threatens to turn vicious, pitting them both against their community. And a lonely daughter finds herself wandering a village in eastern Nigeria in an ill-fated quest, struggling to come to terms with her mother's mental illness.

In ten vivid, evocative stories set in contemporary Nigeria, Uche Okonkwo's *A Kind of Madness* unravels the tensions between mothers and daughters, husbands and wives, best friends, siblings, and more, marking the arrival of an extraordinary new talent in fiction and inviting us all to consider the question: why is it that the people and places we hold closest are so often the ones that drive us to madness?

"Steady-handed and gut-punching. I'm in awe of this mad collection, this necessary writer." —NOVIOLET BULAWAYO, author of *Glory*

"I have no words for what I felt upon reading that last story, that last page. What an accomplishment this book is. *A Kind of Madness* depicts the idiosyncrasies and minutiae of everyday Nigerian life with a careful eye that respects their said idiosyncrasies as worthy of attention, of chronicling, of reinventing. Uche Okonkwo's language is sinuous, maneuvering the reader through stories with a clear-eyed pragmatism and a masterful, often hilarious, use of irony. Her eye is both generous and discerning, and her careful attention asks the reader: won't you see them clearly, too? Marvelous." —LESLEY NNEKA ARIMAH, author of *What It Means When a Man Falls from the Sky*

"In *A Kind of Madness*, Okonkwo casts a critical eye on family and friendships, the ineptness of parents, how the West encroaches on everyday life in Nigeria, the contradictions of chicken as a named entity and chicken in a pepper soup pot. While each story is a world of its own, the collection is at once hilarious and heartbreaking. This is a delightful debut. Congratulations to Uche." —JENNIFER NANSUBUGA MAKUMBI, author of *A Girl is a Body of Water*

"Uche Okonkwo's voice is absorbing. I was immersed in the familiar world of these tender, playfully haunting, darkly funny stories. Okonkwo is a writer to watch." —CHINELO OKPARANTA, author of *Harry Sylvester Bird*

"To read Uche Okonkwo's *A Kind of Madness* is to have an experience: of complex characters grappling with life's many troubles, of a robust culture, of history, of the battle between the domestic and the public, and all the big themes of life woven together. Like Jhumpa Lahiri, Okonkwo's mastery of the form is as rich as some of the short story's best practitioners and deserves every recognition it is sure to get."

—CHIGOZIE OBIOMA,
author of *An Orchestra of Minorities*

"A collection of bangers with protags who run up against and redefine Nigerian society. Lost count of how many times I said hmmm and touched my heart. Uche Okonkwo's stories are among the very best." —SIDIK FOFANA,
author of *Stories from the Tenants Downstairs*

"Uche Okonkwo's *A Kind of Madness* is full of vivid, unforgettable characters and rare insight. This is a book that pulls you in, with its fierce undertow, and once you start reading, you won't want to stop. Okonkwo is one of the most exciting young writers working today, and these stories are brilliant."

—ELLIOTT HOLT,
author of *You Are One of Them*

"Uche Okonkwo's stories, set in contemporary Nigeria, have a gentle allure, drawing us into the intimate lives of characters and their worlds with elegant, assured prose and a deep understanding of the complex machinations of human manners and sentiment. A striking debut!" —KWAME DAWES,
author of *Sturge Town*

A KIND OF MADNESS

STORIES

UCHE OKONKWO

TIN HOUSE / PORTLAND, OREGON

Stories from this collection have appeared in the following literary journals and books, often in earlier form: "Nwunye Belgium" (published as "Our Belgian Wife") in *One Story* and reprinted in *The Best American Nonrequired Reading*, edited by Edan Lepucki, Mariner Books, 2019; "Shadow" in *Ember*; "Long Hair" in *Per Contra*; "Animals" in *ZYZZYVA*; "The Harvest" (published as "Harvesters") in *A Public Space*; "Eden" in *Lagos Noir*, edited by Chris Abani, Akashic Books, 2018; "The Girl Who Lied" in *Ploughshares*; and "Burning" in the *Kenyon Review*.

First US Edition 2024
Printed in the United States of America

Manufacturing by Sheridan
Interior design by Beth Steidle

Library of Congress Cataloging-in-Publication Data

Names: Okonkwo, Uche, 1988- author.
Title: A kind of madness : stories / Uche Okonkwo.
Description: Portland, Oregon : Tin House, 2024.
Identifiers: LCCN 2023046207 | ISBN 9781959030386
(paperback) | ISBN 9781959030539 (ebook)
Subjects: LCSH: Psychological fiction, Nigerian (English) |
Nigeria—Fiction. | LCGFT: Psychological fiction. | Short stories.
Classification: LCC PR9387.9.O378496 K56 2024 |
DDC 823/.92—dc23/eng/20231023
LC record available at https://lccn.loc.gov/2023046207

Tin House
2617 NW Thurman Street, Portland, OR 97210
www.tinhouse.com

DISTRIBUTED BY W. W. NORTON & COMPANY

1 2 3 4 5 6 7 8 9 0

CONTENTS

A KIND OF MADNESS

NWUNYE BELGIUM

UDOKA WAS DISAPPOINTED TO FIND THAT HER PROSPEC-
tive in-laws' house wasn't two stories tall, with a uniformed
guard and a big gate to keep out prying eyes. But though not
as impressive as Udoka had imagined, it was still a better house
than her mother's. It was painted, for one, and the corrugated
roof wasn't coming apart with rust.

Udoka understood exactly what this visit was. When her
mother had come home two weeks ago from her trip to Orlu,
where she'd attended the burial of a distant relative, singing
about God's rain of blessings, Udoka had known that something very good had happened.

"You remember my friend Marigold, who lives in Orlu?"
her mother began as she unpacked her bag. "I went to visit her
and she told me something."

Udoka waited as her mother took out yet another item
from her bag: a kitchen towel, a souvenir from the funeral. She
handed it to Udoka.

"What did she tell you, Mama?" Udoka finally asked.

"She told me her son is looking for a wife," her mother said
with a grin. "The same son that went to Belgium—fifteen years
ago? Yes, in 1982, I remember. Marigold told me that her people were thinking of coming here to Umueze to talk to Gloria's

family, to ask for Gloria's hand for her son. So I told her, I said, 'Gloria? My sister, don't try it o. That girl is public property. Ask anybody in Umueze. That's why no man has come to ask for her hand.'"

Udoka chuckled. "Mama, you didn't have to say that."

"But it's no secret. Everybody in this village knows about Gloria." Her mother leaned forward. "Besides, why send a fine man like my friend's son to another girl's house when you are here?"

Udoka frowned. "But Mama, what about—"

"Wait, let me finish. I told Marigold, I said, 'Don't talk to Gloria's people, my sister. You don't want a prostitute for a daughter-in-law.' And when it was almost time for me to leave, ask me what I did."

"What did you do?"

"I acted as if I just remembered. I said, 'Ah, my daughter sends her greetings. You remember my Udoka? She is now in her second year at Awka Polytechnic.' And she said, 'Oh, tiny Udoka of those days. She must be a big girl now.' Then when she was seeing me off, she said, 'But wait, Agatha. Why can't my son marry your Udoka?'"

"Was she serious, Mama?"

"She was. But you know me, I acted as if it had not even entered my mind. I said, 'That's a very good idea. Let me go home and talk with her.' And that was how it happened."

Udoka shifted her weight from one foot to the other.

"It's a good thing you convinced me to go to this burial, Udoka. If I hadn't gone to Orlu, we would have missed this blessing. See how God works!"

"But Mama, what about Enyinna?"

"What about Enyinna?"

"You know he said he will soon come with his people to discuss my bride price."

"After all these months?" Agatha said. "Forget Enyinna. My friend's son, Uzor, he is a doctor, and he lives in Belgium. You want to compare that to a wretched trader at Onitsha Main Market?"

"Wretched, Mama? His shop is doing okay."

"Ehn, you have said it: 'His shop is doing *okay*.'"

Udoka winced at her mother's deliberately bad impression of her voice.

"You want to manage with a trader that is 'doing okay,' a man who drives a rotten matchbox and calls it a car, when you can marry a doctor making big money in Belgium?"

Udoka considered this. Enyinna was a fine man, but he was no doctor and definitely not a Belgian one. He had never even been outside of the country and had said many times that he had no interest in pursuing a university degree—something that had never bothered Udoka until now.

"But—so what will we tell Enyinna and his family? And even our umunna?" Udoka said. "Won't it be a shame to—"

"Udoka, leave shame to its owners. Think about your own life. When Marigold's son marries you, he will take you to Belgium. You will leave that stupid Awka Polytechnic, where the lecturers are always on strike. When you go to Belgium, you will attend a proper school!"

Udoka chewed her lower lip. "That's true," she said. "They have good schools in Belgium."

"Of course! And guess who will be paying your fees?"

Udoka started to speak, but her mother's pause lasted only a second.

"Your husband! And when you finish school, you won't even have to work if you don't want to. You can just relax and let your husband take care of you. And you know they don't have sun in those places like Belgium, so your body will be very fresh. By the time you come back to visit me ehn, this your skin that was yellow before, it will be shining white like that of an oyibo. And you will be talking like them, *shiriri, shiriri,* as if you are holding water in your mouth. And all these bush village people of Umueze will not be able to understand what you are saying, and they will be asking, 'Is that Udoka? The same Udoka of yesterday?' And I will say, 'Yes, yes, that is my Udoka.'" Agatha laughed, clapping her hands with delight. "And Uzor will be sending me plenty of dollars, and I will expand my shop and hire girls to work for me. And I will campaign for the head of the women's group of Umueze, and they will be looking at me every time from the corners of their eyes, because I am the only one of them to have a daughter that lives in obodo-oyibo Belgium."

Udoka watched her mother's face soften into a dreamy, faraway look, one she imagined her mother had worn a lot more before her father's death and the hardships that followed. When her mother gave her a conspiratorial nudge, Udoka responded with a smile.

Udoka's mother had spent the next few days preparing her for the visit, telling her all the things that Marigold would be looking for. Marigold, like any mother-in-law, would want to see that Udoka could take care of a home. She would want to know if Udoka was modest and submissive, or if she was the kind who would want to seize her husband's trousers and wear them. Marigold had said she had a preference for light-skinned girls like Udoka; she wanted a daughter-in-law she could brag about and call nwanyi-ocha, fair lady. It was also a good thing Udoka was not too thin—Marigold didn't like "toothpicks."

. . .

UDOKA SMOOTHED DOWN THE FRONT of her skirt with shaky hands. Her palms were damp with sweat. She stood still and girded herself as her mother gave her a final once-over. "Perfect," her mother said, placing a finger on Udoka's chin and gently lifting her face. Udoka felt a surge of warmth in her chest.

Agatha knocked and the door opened. Marigold's massive frame appeared in the doorway.

"Agatha, Udoka, our daughter, welcome." She stepped forward to embrace first Agatha and then Udoka.

Marigold led her guests into the living room, where her husband, Mazi Okoro—appearing comically small beside her—set aside his newspaper and rose from his chair. He greeted Udoka and her mother with a smile, peering at them through the thick lenses of his glasses as he asked polite questions about their journey and life in Umueze. Udoka found herself slightly disappointed with the living room. The paint on the walls was fresh and unmarked, but the furniture, though sturdy-looking, was faded. The room was decorated with artificial plants, and an old family photo showing Marigold, Mazi Okoro, and their son, Uzor, hung on a wall. Udoka squinted at the photo, hoping to see something of the man she would marry in the scrawny boy.

Udoka and her mother sat on the mud-colored sofa across from Mazi Okoro, and Marigold took the vacant chair beside her husband. Conscious of her every move being watched, Udoka was careful to appear shy (a sure sign of modesty), smiling and averting her eyes each time Marigold or her husband complimented her on her skin or her manners. She could tell that Marigold approved of her attire of an ankle-length skirt and a top with sleeves long enough to cover her elbows. Her mother had made her take out her hair extensions and wear her

God-given hair in plaits, and when Mazi Okoro made a joke about women who went into hair salons looking like humans only to come out looking like Ekpo masquerades, Udoka knew it had been a wise decision.

After a while, Marigold served steaming wraps of okpa on a large platter. "Just something small to hold our stomachs until I prepare lunch," she said as she set it down on the center table. Udoka relished the firmness of the okpa, the way the spices came together in her mouth—the pepper sharp enough to sting but not hot enough to catch in her throat. The palm oil was the good kind; it didn't leave a gritty feeling on the roof of her mouth. Marigold would expect the same level of culinary excellence from a daughter-in-law.

When they finished the okpa, Marigold invited Udoka into the kitchen to help with lunch, telling Agatha to rest in the guest bedroom. Udoka recognized this as a ploy to get her alone, and she felt suddenly grateful for all the cooking lessons her mother had subjected her to as a girl. She would be on her best behavior. Her future, and her mother's, depended on it.

Marigold's kitchen was impressively modern to Udoka, with its terrazzo floor, tiled counters, and gleaming stainless-steel sink with running water. There was also a gas cooker, which spurted a cool blue flame when Marigold turned it on. Udoka tried to keep her eyes from widening in appreciation. She was not sure how much Marigold knew of her family's financial situation, especially since her father's death eleven years ago, but she didn't want her potential mother-in-law thinking she and her mother were undeserving of her sophisticated son. She wondered what Marigold would think when she visited their house and saw the extent of her family's decline. She was particularly ashamed of the old mud structure that stood at the back of the compound and served as a kitchen, with its walls blackened from smoke, the firewood smell that clung to one's clothes, and the lizards playing endless games of hide-and-seek in the rafters.

Udoka reminded herself to focus on the tasks at hand. She needed to make a good impression today so Marigold would overlook anything she might consider less than ideal about Udoka and her mother's status.

"What are we making, Mama?" Udoka asked.

"Egusi soup. It's Mazi Okoro's favorite."

As they worked, Udoka felt Marigold watching her, noting how thoroughly she washed the meat and cleaned the tripe and cow skin. Marigold measured with her eyes how much spice and seasoning Udoka used, how high she set the fire to cook the meat. Marigold, smiling and disingenuous, kept assigning the more difficult tasks to Udoka. When Marigold placed a bowl of live, unshelled periwinkles before her, Udoka tried not to show her distress.

"Mazi Okoro likes periwinkles in his soup," Marigold said.

Udoka swallowed. She had never handled unshelled periwinkles. Her mother, whenever she bought periwinkles, had them shelled at the market. In her panic, she asked what she thought was a stupid question.

"Should I remove them from the shells, Mama?"

"No, my dear. Just break off the tail end. Use this." Marigold took a small machete from a drawer and handed it to Udoka. "My husband likes to suck the periwinkles out of the shells."

Marigold gave her a low stool to sit on and spread a few newspaper pages on the floor, so she could break off the shells without scarring it. She said, "Make sure you don't cut too much or too little off the shell. If you cut too much, the periwinkle will fall out; cut too little, and it will be impossible to suck it from the shell."

Udoka took the first periwinkle between her thumb and index finger, held it to the floor, said a silent prayer, and brought the machete down hard on the pointed end. The end came off with a satisfying snap, and Udoka hid her relief. Marigold watched her work on a few more periwinkles, nodding her approval before turning away to check on the meat.

With the periwinkles cut and washed several times over, Udoka heated palm oil in a pot on the stove while Marigold pretended to arrange her shelves. Udoka added the onions that Marigold had chopped, fragrant steam from the pot enveloping her face and filling the room. With the onions frying, Udoka poured in the ground melon seeds Marigold had measured out, stirring the yellow paste to keep it from burning. She tasted the mixture after a while, remembering to put the ladle to her palm and not her tongue. When the melon seeds had fried long enough, Udoka added the meats and stock, tasted the mixture again, added some more pepper, salt, seasoning cubes, and crayfish, covered the pot, and left it to simmer. She would add the periwinkles later and, finally, when the pot was almost ready to come off the stove, the ugu leaves.

With most of the cooking done, Udoka started to tidy up the kitchen, gathering the dirty utensils into the sink and filling a bowl with water from the tap. There was no running water in her mother's house, and so Udoka enjoyed this, the way the tap sputtered to life and let out a stream of sun-warmed water when she turned its head.

Marigold cleared her throat, startling Udoka. She looked up from the sink to find Marigold standing very close.

"My dear," Marigold said quietly, "I want to ask you something."

"Yes, Mama?"

"Are you—?" She gave Udoka's crotch a meaningful look. "When my son knocks at the door, will he meet you at home?"

Udoka looked away—it was the reaction expected from any decent girl when topics like this were raised. She contemplated the dishwashing water. There had been that one boy when she was in her first year at Awka Poly, that one evening, with her panties down and him panting on top of her. "Just the tip. Let me put just the tip," he'd croaked, his eyes bulging like he was choking to death. She had let him (but just the tip), and moments later he shuddered his release, and she shoved him off her so she could look, with dread, for any sign of red on his off-white sheets. There had been nothing, and therefore she could say the words with a clear conscience.

"Yes, Mama. I am a virgin."

"Hewu!" Marigold cried, enfolding Udoka in her arms. "My daughter, you have made me very happy. I didn't think I could find a virgin wife for my Uzor; you know how girls are these days, not like when your mother and I were young. I thank God for my friend Agatha, for bringing you for my son!"

Udoka started to smile, but then she remembered how attractive a little insecurity could be. She lowered her gaze to the floor. "But, Mama, what if Uzor doesn't like me?"

"What do you mean he won't like you?" Marigold scolded gently. "What else can my son be looking for? Beautiful nwanyi-ocha like you, modest and intelligent. I know a good thing, and so does my son. If he does not marry you, it means he won't marry at all."

Udoka allowed herself a small smile. Her mother would be proud.

. . .

IT HAD BEEN JUST OVER a week since the visit to her new in-laws, and Udoka was happy. If she didn't have her Belgian doctor, she would have been worried: about the academic staff at her school, who were still on their months-long "indefinite" strike; about her mother having to borrow money from the women's cooperative from time to time to keep her in school. But her Belgian doctor had erased the creases on her forehead. She was in such high spirits that, at the market a few minutes ago, it had been impossible for her to curse back at the butcher when he'd insulted her for haggling too low. "Carry your bad luck and leave my stall!" he'd yelled, waving his knife. Bad luck? Udoka laughed. Bad luck did not fetch one a husband from Belgium.

After their return from Orlu, Udoka had watched her mother, with a feeling of awe and mild unease, as she set about dismantling the wedding plans with Enyinna's family, like a God-ordained whirlwind. Within a few days, Agatha had arranged a meeting with both families to call the wedding off. It didn't matter that Enyinna's family was shocked and upset, or that Enyinna, who lived and worked in Onitsha, was yet to be informed of the new developments. With the news broken to Enyinna's family, Agatha had gone ahead and set up a date with the umunna—agreed upon by her, Marigold, and Mazi Okoro—in the coming week for Marigold's family to make their marriage request official. When this was done, and the umunna gave consent, the way would be paved for the bride price negotiation and then the wedding proper. Marigold had said Uzor would be visiting Nigeria in about three weeks, and once he arrived in Orlu, things would move even quicker. Udoka was more than ready to leave what she considered her old life behind. Her mother, in addition to handling the breakup, had spread the word of her daughter's new suitor all around Umueze, so that some people had begun calling Udoka "Nwunye Belgium"—Belgium wife—telling her to remember them when she entered into her obodo-oyibo paradise.

So far, since the breakup, Udoka had succeeded, through careful effort, in avoiding Enyinna's family around the village. She had begun making her daily trips to the water pump in the afternoons, when the sun was at its fieriest and she was least likely to run into other people out fetching water. Each time Udoka visited her mother's tailoring shop, she would take a circuitous route of narrow footpaths, sometimes cutting through private backyards and gardens, just so she could stay off the main road and avoid Enyinna's family house. Now, on her way back from the village market, she walked quickly and stayed alert, prepared to duck behind a tree or a fence if she saw one of Enyinna's people. She wondered if Enyinna had heard the news yet. She told herself that when the inevitable confrontation came, she would face him, bold and unwavering. Because, given the choice, anyone would do as she had.

Udoka swung her bag of foodstuff back and forth and skipped lightly as she turned onto her street, pleased to have avoided her ex-fiancé's family for another day. The road was unpaved, and a small cloud of red dust rose from the ground with every step she took. In Belgium, she would walk on real roads.

Udoka heard a car behind her and stepped closer to the shoulder of the road. But then, recognizing the familiar rattling of the vehicle's engine, she glanced back. Enyinna's brown Volvo, scarred and dented, was unmistakable. Udoka quickened her pace.

"Udoka."

She walked faster, her eyes fixed ahead, ignoring the car now beside her.

"Udoka, wait!"

Udoka ran, her feet pounding the ground. When she caught sight of the mango tree that marked the entrance to her mother's compound, she ran even faster. The car's horn blared, shrill and grating on the quiet street. Udoka pretended there was no Enyinna, no clattering hulk of metal keeping pace beside her, no neighbors following her with keen eyes.

Udoka threw open her mother's squeaky gate and stumbled through. Her mother was bent over the large water drum beside the house with a scooping bowl and a bucket. She straightened up at once.

"Udoka, what is chasing you?"

Udoka ran past her mother and into the house, bolting the front door behind her and leaning against it as she took gasping breaths. Soon enough, she heard the squeaking of the gate again, and then: "Udoka! Udoka, why are you running from me?"

"Enyinna, why do you want to bring down my roof with your screaming?" Udoka heard her mother say. With shaky limbs, she got on her knees and crept to the living room window. She lifted a corner of the frayed curtain to look outside.

Enyinna, his tone somewhat indignant, said, "Sorry, Mama. I didn't see you there."

"It's not your fault," Agatha said, "since I'm now invisible. What do you want?"

"Mama, they told me you brought your people to cancel the wedding—"

"And?"

"Is it true?"

"It is true. Did they also tell you that a doctor from Belgium is coming to marry my daughter?"

Udoka winced. Her mother's back was turned, so Udoka could not see her face. But she could decode her mother's expression from Enyinna's, like some kind of mirror in reverse. Hurt and anger on Enyinna's face, defiance and mockery on her mother's. She rubbed her wet palms over her churning stomach.

Kneeling there behind the curtain, Udoka wondered how different things might have been had her father not died. More than even her grief, it was the burden of holding the family together that had torn at her mother. Udoka's family had never been wealthy, but with her father's teacher's salary and her mother's tailoring business, they had gotten by. In the years following her father's death, her mother had grown harder, inside and out: more controlling as her hands grew calloused from overworking; more critical as worry lines emerged on her forehead; more materialistic even as their house crumbled under the weight of repairs they could not afford to make.

As a teenager, Udoka had witnessed creditors accost her mother at home and in public, with curses and, in one case, a policeman. Too many times she'd had to avert her eyes or sneak away so she wouldn't have to see her mother beg for "just one more week," wouldn't have to endure her mother's attempts to reassert her authority at home by being even harder on Udoka than she already was. And so as much as she hated hurting Enyinna this way, Udoka knew the doctor from Belgium was the better choice, because her mother deserved some relief from a life of want, because Udoka herself did not want to live like this forever.

"So it's true," Enyinna said. His face was to the ground, his voice so quiet Udoka had to strain to hear. "I didn't want to believe—"

Udoka felt her throat tighten. Her mother resumed filling her bucket from the water drum.

Enyinna's voice was hoarse when he spoke next. "Mama, please—"

"Enyinna, the family and umunna have accepted Udoka's new husband. Very soon he will come and pay her bride price, and they will do the wine carrying. You had Udoka for almost a year, yet you kept dragging your feet."

"But Mama, it was never like that," Enyinna said, in that high-pitched tone he used when trying to make a case. "Udoka deserves the best. I needed the time to gather enough money so I could give her a correct bride price and a fine wedding. I explained to you, Mama, and you said you understood. I am ready now. I will marry Udoka today if—"

"Enyinna," Agatha said, her voice falsely sweet, "you know the one thing you have said today that makes sense? 'Udoka deserves the best.' And she has it now. Be happy for her. Let God have His way."

"Let God have His way?" Enyinna said. "So you are saying this is God's will because the man has more money than me."

All the while Agatha had carried on filling her bucket. She stopped now, straightening up to look at Enyinna. "More?" Agatha's voice was soft, and Udoka could tell her mother's face would be wearing that look of exaggerated confusion she feigned so well. "But Enyinna, what money did you ever have in the first place?"

This was her mother's final blow. Proud Igbo man that Enyinna was, there could be no greater gratification than seeing his family well taken care of, protected from a life of want, and no greater shame than being perceived as incapable of doing so.

Enyinna walked away without another word. Udoka listened to his matchbox car rattle down the street.

. . .

THE FIRST TIME UDOKA HEARD the snickering behind her, she was certain it wasn't at her expense. She knew that sound well, could read the mockery in it like a book. She had made that sound at people before, when she was, like these young women—no, girls—frivolous and immature.

Udoka liked the burden of responsibility on her soon-to-be-married shoulders. She liked that it was no longer proper for her to spend too much time with her single Umueze counterparts. With Marigold having sent word three weeks ago that Uzor had arrived in Orlu, it was important that she didn't give the gossip mongers a reason to start even the smallest rumor about her. Most of the pre-wedding matters—the official marriage proposal, the acceptance, and the checking into each family's background for deal-breakers ranging from epilepsy to serious criminal behavior—had been finalized before Uzor's arrival. All that was left was negotiating and paying the bride price, and then the wedding.

This man, Uzor, was all Udoka could think about. The lecturers' strike had ended a week ago and school had reopened, but it didn't matter now. Udoka had returned to campus merely to invite her friends to her wedding and empty out her hostel room. She knew she would not be returning.

Udoka wondered what her husband was like. He would no longer talk like an Igbo man, she was sure. Maybe he wouldn't even remember how to speak Igbo, or he would speak it with a strange accent that would make everyone smile and indulge him. Would he still eat fufu with his hands or, as she hoped, with a fork and knife? And surely, he would be a gentleman, like the men she saw in oyibo films, men who helped with housework and brought their wives breakfast in bed.

The girls giggled again, and now it took a lot of resolve for Udoka not to look in the direction of their laughter and ask what had happened. She would bide her time. She was next in the queue for the water pump. When it was her turn, she would place her bucket under the nozzle and, when she turned around to use the hand-operated pump, she would smile at the girls and ask, with a carefully constructed air of disinterest, why they were laughing.

When Udoka got behind the pump and regarded the three laughing girls like she had planned, she was surprised at the effort they put into straightening their faces. If she'd been uncertain of her new status in Umueze, she would have felt self-conscious.

"How are you girls?" she asked.

"We girls are fine," the one called Chisom answered. Udoka recognized the other two but didn't know their names.

"What's making you laugh?" Udoka said, concentrating on raising and lowering the pump's handle to let out water.

"Nothing," said Chisom, clearly the mouthpiece of the group.

It dawned on Udoka that they realized she was no longer one of them, and that was why they were reluctant to share their gossip with her. Fair enough. She needed to make more friends from among her equals anyway.

"Nwunye Belgium," Chisom said, "when is your husband coming to Umueze?" Chisom's voice was low, her concern clearly insincere. "Or aren't you going to Belgium anymore?"

Udoka frowned. "What kind of question is that? Of course he is coming, very soon."

"Okay o," Chisom said. "I said I should ask because I visited my cousin in Orlu the other day, and I asked if she'd heard about the big wedding that's about to happen, but she was arguing with me—"

"Arguing about what?" Udoka asked.

The other girls averted their faces, but Udoka could see their shoulders tremble as they chuckled. Only then did Udoka start to wonder. The suppressed laughter, the look of exaggerated innocence and concern on Chisom's face, her tone at once

16

mocking and deferential. Udoka felt her grip on the pump's handle slacken. Thankfully, her bucket was full.

"Nothing, don't mind me." Chisom's voice retained its sweetness. "It's just that we have been waiting so long to see this our husband, and now people are starting to spread rumors. But we are all very happy for you. We pray for your kind of luck."

"God forbid!"

Udoka wasn't sure which of the other girls had muttered it, but it didn't matter. She needed to leave at once and find out what these girls thought they knew. She stepped from behind the pump to lift her bucket onto her head.

"No, no, no, Nwunye Belgium, let me help you," Chisom said, rushing forward. "You know we need to keep you fresh for our husband when he finally comes."

Udoka was speechless as Chisom lifted the bucket and placed it with exaggerated care on Udoka's head. Udoka walked away from the pump, her hands holding the bucket steady. The girls' laughter followed her, down the footpath and all the way home.

. . .

AGATHA WAS NOT WORRIED. She knew better than silly Udoka, who had come home from the water pump yesterday agitated by something she'd heard and demanding that Agatha immediately visit Marigold in Orlu. People could be vicious, and they would tell all kinds of lies when jealousy was eating them up. The only reason Marigold and her people hadn't shown up yet to finalize the wedding was that they were busy preparing to throw the biggest wedding party in the history of Umueze. She had told her daughter this, but Udoka had been insistent. And so here Agatha was, walking through her friend's compound to the front door.

It was when Agatha reached the threshold, wiping her soles on the foot mat, that she realized something was not quite right. Marigold's house should have been swarming with people eager to "welcome" the doctor from Belgium, in the hopes of leaving with gifts from him. There should have been extended family and neighbors offering help so they would find favor with their wealthy relative. But Agatha calmed herself with the thought that she must have arrived at a rare quiet moment, and worried instead that she might be interrupting her in-laws' rest. She knocked.

"Who is there?" Marigold's voice called from within.

"It's your in-law, Agatha."

After a minute, the door swung open and Agatha smiled at her friend. Marigold did not return the smile. Marigold's demeanor surprised Agatha, but she continued with a cheerful voice. "How are you, Marigold? I said let me come and see how my people are doing today."

"We are fine," Marigold said, stepping aside from the doorway with clear reluctance.

They walked together into the living room and sat. Marigold said nothing, so Agatha filled the silence with complaints about the bad state of the roads and the stress of the journey. All the while, Agatha wondered why her friend was acting like someone had poured cold water over her body.

After another long silence, Agatha said with an uncomfortable laugh, "Marigold, won't you offer me something to drink?"

"We have only water."

Agatha's sense of unease deepened. She forced a smile through the panic starting to rise in her throat.

"Why is your face like stone?" she asked. "If I didn't know better, I would have thought you don't want me in your house. Please, call my son-in-law so I can finally meet him."

"Which son-in-law?"

Agatha recoiled at Marigold's sharp tone. "Your son, Uzor," she said. "Why are you talking like this?"

"Why am I talking like this? Agatha, I have found your secret," Marigold said, leaning forward to point an index finger in Agatha's face. "The breeze has blown, and we have now seen the anus of the fowl!"

Agatha shifted to perch on the edge of her seat. "What secret? I don't have any secret."

"Oh, so you just forgot to mention that you people have mental illness in your family," Marigold said.

Agatha sprang to her feet. "That's not true! Marigold, why would you say something like that? You know my family very well. Where is this coming from?"

Marigold stood. "All we know is that after we thought the checking of your family's background was done, one of our old uncles told us that your grandmother had a great-aunt who went mad. So you people thought that because it was a long time ago, nobody would remember? God has exposed you!"

"It's a lie!"

"So now you are calling our uncle a liar?"

Agatha opened her mouth to protest, but Marigold carried on.

"Anyway, let us stop wasting each other's time. My son has already gone back to Belgium."

"Without even seeing my Udoka?"

"What is there to see? The woman he came to marry is from a family of mad people, so he went back to Belgium. Simple."

Agatha stood quiet for a moment, and then she said, "If your son doesn't want to get married anymore, why not just admit it, instead of making up such a big lie about my family? Do you know how many men were lining up at my door to marry Udoka? She left a very successful businessman to marry your son!"

Marigold's laughter dripped with scorn. "I wish you and your many suitors all the best," she said. "It is only mad people that look for other mad people to marry. We will come and see your umunna and tell them the wedding is canceled. You and your daughter can do whatever you want."

"Better come quickly!" Agatha said. "My daughter was not lacking suitors before your son. I just thought it would be good for our children to marry because we were friends. Now you are putting shame on my family, but it is God who will judge you. Just use your conscience, and don't go around telling people there is madness in my family."

"I have heard you," Marigold said. "Now please carry your madness and leave my house."

Agatha walked to the door on shaky legs.

. . .

MARIGOLD SLAMMED THE DOOR, locked it, and bent to watch through the keyhole. When Agatha was gone, Marigold let out a sigh, ignoring the twinge of guilt in her heart.

As she reentered the living room, her husband emerged from their bedroom.

"I see you're done hiding," Marigold said.

"And I see you decided to go with the madness story."

"It's not like you had a better idea."

"It was your idea to set up this whole wedding thing in the first place when nobody asked you."

"Ehn, go ahead and blame me for trying to help."

"Trying to help who?"

Marigold glared at her husband. "You're talking as if you don't live in this same town. I don't know how it is for you men, but me, all I hear these days is, 'Oh my son is getting married';

20

'Oh my daughter just gave birth, I am going for omugwo.' I can't go anywhere without someone asking about Uzor. 'When will he marry? When will we rub powder for your own grand-child? Is everything okay? Should we be praying?' One day, we will wake up and people will have answered all these questions for themselves. And you know how that goes."

It was decades ago now, but the memory was still sharp for both of them: those long years of waiting and trying before they had Uzor. The rumors had spread like fire: Mazi Okoro was weak; Marigold had tied up his manhood in a bottle; Mari-gold's womb had bitter water and no child could survive in it. Even after Uzor was born, it was a long time before they could stop looking over their shoulders, stop searching for the malice lurking beneath every smile that was offered to them.

They avoided each other's eyes as they sat on opposite ends of the sofa.

"But why is Uzor refusing to get married and settle down, at his age?" Marigold said, as much to herself as to her husband. "There's something he is not telling us."

They let the silence sit with them for a while, and both finally agreed, with themselves and with each other, that no, their Uzor could not be one of those homosexuals they kept hearing about. They had raised him well. Perhaps there was some oyibo girl in Belgium who had caught his eye. Marigold and Mazi Okoro had always insisted on Uzor coming home to take a wife; they would not accept some strange girl whose family and history they did not know. But with their son now nearing forty, an oyibo daughter-in-law might not be the worst thing in the world.

It still seemed like yesterday to Marigold when her Uzor, her doctor-in-the-making, had come home from university to inform her and Mazi Okoro that he, along with two friends, had put together enough money to travel abroad to Belgium. With nothing more by way of a plan, the boys had set off, Uzor ignoring his parents' pleas and threats of disownment. It would be two years before they heard from him again, via a letter saying he was fine, he was starting a business. In the meantime, when people asked about her son, Marigold said he'd gone to Belgium to complete his medical degree. It would be another couple of years before Uzor began sending money home, money he claimed he was making from "imports and exports." That was the extent of Marigold and Mazi Okoro's knowledge of Uzor's career; the two previous times he'd visited home, he'd been as vague and tight-lipped about his work as he was in his letters.

"There are many things he is not telling us." Mazi Okoro sighed. "You know Agatha's family will not accept this madness business."

"They don't have to accept it, and we don't have to prove anything. It's just a matter of whose story is sweeter and who can make more noise. Me, I've already started."

Mazi Okoro eyed his wife. "This woman, I fear you sometimes."

"Oh, so you would prefer that people talk about us instead of them?"

. . .

UDOKA AND HER MOTHER SAT in the shade of the veranda in front of their house, sifting through a tray of beans and throwing out chaff and small stones. Over a month had gone by since Udoka's engagement to the doctor had ended, yet people still called her "Nwunye Belgium." "Nwunye Belgium," they would call out, ignoring her ignoring them, "you are still with us in Umueze?" Or "Nwunye Belgium, when you go to Belgium, make sure you ask the oyibos if they can cure madness."

Udoka could not believe how quickly things had changed for her. When her mother returned from that last trip to Marigold's house and related the details of the visit, Udoka had seen the life she'd envisioned for herself crumble. She'd spent the next few days huddled in an inconsolable heap in her room, while her mother tried to coax her into normalcy with steaming bowls of pepper soup. Simple tasks like fetching water and going to the market became unbearable, with people giggling and pointing fingers behind her back.

"I saw Mama Enyinna today," her mother said. Udoka knew she was supposed to ask a question, to draw the story out of her mother. She ignored her mother's sidelong glances.

"Did I tell you what she did to me at the last Umueze women's meeting?" her mother eventually said.

"You told me, Mama."

Agatha carried on anyway. "I didn't look for her trouble o. We were discussing what punishment to give to women who don't pay the monthly levy on time, and Mama Caro said that they should be fined two times the fee. So I raised my hand. I said times two was too harsh, that they should just add a small penalty on top of the levy instead, because everybody knows that things are very hard these days. And then Mama Enyinna said, 'I didn't know that things are hard for Belgium people too.' Then she and her friends started to laugh." Agatha put her index finger to her tongue and pointed to the sky. "I swear, I wanted to get up and beat Mama Enyinna very well, use sand to scrub her mouth!"

Udoka kept her eyes on the beans. She wondered what her mother would say if she told her about that afternoon soon after Uzor's family ended the engagement when she'd taken

the two-hour bus ride to Onitsha Main Market. She'd nego-
tiated her way through the narrow corridors with shops on
either side, ignoring the calls and the outstretched hands of
traders trying to get her attention. She found Enyinna sitting
on a stool outside his shop, his shop boy beside him. They
were talking and peering into what appeared to be his stock
book. The shop boy looked up and saw Udoka; he said something to Enyinna. Enyinna raised his head and gave Udoka the
widest smile she had ever seen on him. Udoka smiled back,
hope soaring in her heart. Enyinna sprang from his stool and
rushed to meet her. He took her hand and led her to sit on his
vacated stool.

"Linus!" Enyinna shouted to his shop boy. "Go and collect
a cold bottle of Coke from Mama Doodi's stall. Be quick, ehn!
Nwunye Belgium must be very thirsty after her journey."

The smile grew stiff on Udoka's face. She stood to leave, but
Enyinna blocked her way, lowering her to the stool with his
smile still in place.

"Nwunye Belgium, sit down and rest your feet," he said. His
voice was starting to attract the attention of neighboring shop
owners. "Linus is bringing the Coke. It won't be as sweet as the
kind they have in Belgium, but I hope you can manage it."

Udoka sat, trying to hide her apprehension as she eyed the
other shop owners. She knew most of them from her previous visits. They sold the same kinds of cosmetic products that
Enyinna did, but there was a geniality to their competition,
and Udoka knew he would have told them what she and her
mother had done to him. Any doubts she might have had of this
were dispelled by the hostility she now saw in their faces. They
had always had friendly smiles for her, calling her "our wife,"
making jokes about stealing her from Enyinna, and buying her
plates of abacha from passing hawkers. Today their faces were

hard, their eyes knowing. They started to gather in front of Enyinna's shop.

"See, Nwunye Belgium came to visit us today," Enyinna addressed them.

"But Enyinna," a voice called out, "I thought you said she was going to Belgium with one doctor."

Udoka sat examining her sandaled feet and blinking back tears.

"Yes, but something bad happened," Enyinna said, his voice heavy with feigned sorrow. "The man came from Belgium but refused to marry her. Because they have madness in their family."

Exclamations of "Tufiakwa!" and "Madness?" ripped through the gathered shop owners. Udoka couldn't find her voice to say that the rumors were not true. She didn't think it would matter to the men, or to Enyinna, anyway.

Udoka sprang from the stool, tears falling down her face as she dashed through the crowd, laughter echoing behind her. She cried all the way home, arriving minutes before her mother returned from her shop. Seeing Udoka's swollen face, Agatha assumed she was suffering through another bout of melancholy and sat with her in quiet solidarity. Udoka had let her mother think what she might, convincing herself she was waiting for a good time to tell her about her visit to Enyinna. But now she realized she never would.

"Oh, Udoka my daughter, we have suffered." Agatha turned down her lips and shook her head. "And that Marigold, going about running her diarrhea mouth, telling people there is madness in our family. God will punish her. God will punish all of them."

Listening to her mother rain curses on all the people she believed were out to get them, Udoka wondered if there wasn't some kind of twisted truth to the madness rumors. How else could one explain her mother's stubborn insistence on her own innocence, her willful blindness?

"This is the work of our enemies," Agatha said, nodding slowly. "But don't worry, they will all be put to shame. God will open another door for you. He will bring another good man. A better man!"

Udoka swallowed her exasperation. It *was* madness: her mother's hunger for the kind of salvation that could come only from a man, and Udoka herself, how readily she had surrendered the reins of her life, letting her mother decide how they, how she, should be saved.

"Mama," she said finally, "I want to go back to school. I've missed many weeks already."

"Okay," Agatha said absently. "I'll give you some money from the shop tomorrow. Manage that, you hear?"

"Yes, Mama."

They sat staring ahead, Udoka still while her mother shook her legs and ground her teeth in misery.

"Udoka, I'm telling you, this is the work of our enemies," Agatha said. "But God will fight for us."

Udoka felt her mother reach for her hand and squeeze it tight. She did not squeeze back.

SHADOW

I

BUCHI TOOK A STEP TOWARD AUNTY IFUEKO, CAREFUL not to make a sound. He'd heard her return from the market moments before, with his mother and Aunty Agnes. Now, she was in the kitchen by herself, humming a Christmas tune as she pulled things out of a plastic bag.

He inched forward until he was standing behind her. He inhaled her familiar lemongrass scent, now mixed with the smell of sweat and something vaguely coppery. She turned suddenly, bumping into him but reaching out in time to steady him on his feet.

"Buchi, there you are," she said, with that special smile he knew was for him alone. He was pleased at the breathless surprise in her voice, touched that she'd feigned it for him even though she would not have forgotten his old habit of following her around.

"Nnọọ, Aunty."

Aunty Ifueko laughed. "Look at you, greeting me in Igbo. Soon I'll be taking lessons from you."

Buchi wished his father was within earshot. His father didn't spend much time at home, but the fog of his disapproval hung low and heavy around the house even when he wasn't there. If

27

he'd heard Aunty Ifueko's words, maybe he would have smiled, praised Buchi for his effort. But Buchi knew better. His father was not a man who gave grace easily.

Buchi's father liked to say that language was part of the "great heritage of Ndigbo," of which he was determined his children, Buchi and his older sister, Chinelo, would partake. And so, even though he'd barred his wife from speaking Igbo with the children at home—terrified that their English would be tainted—he would, every so often, engage Buchi and Chinelo in sporadic Igbo language and culture lessons that sometimes ended with Buchi close to tears. Unlike Chinelo, Buchi was never able to distinguish between all the ways of pronouncing the word "akwa"—each of which meant a different thing in English: *bed*, *cloth*, *egg*, *tears*—no matter how many times his father pointed out high versus low pitch, his voice taking up so much space it became a fourth presence in the room. When the lessons were over, his father's disappointed gaze would follow Buchi around like a bad smell.

Aunty Ifueko never looked at Buchi with disappointment. She looked at him like they shared a funny secret she was always on the verge of laughing about. It was a tragedy, a great injustice, that he only got to see her every December, when his father's siblings, Uncle Michael and Aunty Agnes, traveled to Lagos to spend the holidays with them, Uncle Michael flying in from New Jersey with Aunty Ifueko, his wife, and Aunty Agnes driving down from Aba, where she lived with her son, Ogo.

"I've given Chinelo and Ogo their goodies, but don't think I forgot you," Aunty Ifueko said, tugging playfully on the soft flesh of his cheek. "How can I forget my own shadow?"

Buchi chuckled. The thought of being Aunty Ifueko's shadow still tickled him, even though that joke was now old. It was his mother who'd started it, after she noticed how Buchi clung to Aunty Ifueko. "Ifueko," she'd said, "how come you have a shadow that doesn't match your body?" Buchi had been six then, and he'd thought it was the coolest thing, being his aunty's shadow. So he took it upon himself to become the embodiment of the name, sneaking behind Aunty Ifueko, laughing out loud when she turned around to find him there and put her hand over her heart. He could have kept up with their special game forever, but Ogo began teasing him relentlessly whenever there were no adults around to hear. "You look like a kitten crying for his mummy's breast milk," Ogo would say.

Still, Buchi found ways to be around Aunty Ifueko, determined every December to make the most of their short time together. He would make his way past the backyard to the refurbished boys' quarters—a small building behind the house with a bedroom, a bathroom, and a kitchenette the size of a closet, originally built for live-in help—where Aunty Ifueko and her husband stayed during their visits. He'd sit with her in the bedroom, and they'd sort and wrap the gifts she and Uncle Michael had bought for everyone. She would tell him about snowy winters, and he'd imagine himself eating the white flakes straight from the sky.

Aunty Ifueko lifted a Mr. Bigg's bag from the counter. She took out a doughnut and handed it to Buchi. And even though he knew it was the exact same kind of doughnut Aunty Ifueko had given his sister and cousin just minutes ago, this one was different. This doughnut was warmer, its smell richer. Buchi knew that when he bit into the middle, the strawberry jam he tasted would be redder and sweeter than anything in the whole world.

"Thank you, Aunty," he said.

Aunty Ifueko turned back to the kitchen counter, telling Buchi about the trip to the market, how the prices of everything

had gone up. Buchi took in her words with large bites of doughnut, crunching sugar between his teeth while she removed food
items from her plastic bags: lettuce and cabbages and cucum-
bers, ugu leaves, two large smoked fish coiled into circles, their
tails tucked into open mouths, a bunch of plantains as long as
his arm. Aunty Ifueko put the ugu leaves in a bowl and placed it
beneath the tap. She began rinsing. He carried a low stool over
to the sink and got on top of it.

"Can you finish washing the ugu while I start on the plantains?" Aunty Ifueko asked.

"Yes, Aunty," he said. Like he could ever say no to her.

"Good boy."

She took her wet hands out of the bowl and, before turning
away from the sink, patted Buchi's head. A drop of water slid
down his forehead and rolled between his eyes. He watched it
disappear down the bridge of his nose, then opened his mouth
and caught it.

Buchi had just finished washing the ugu leaves when he
heard footsteps approaching the kitchen. He knew the sound of
those feet, loud and commanding as if they had a score to settle
with the ground.

"*Kpom kpom kpom.*" The playfulness in Aunty Agnes's voice
belied her entire persona. "Who is here?"

"In the kitchen," Aunty Ifueko called out. Buchi wanted
to jump from his stool, slam the kitchen door shut, and lock it.
Then he would laugh at Aunty Agnes struggling on the other
side, her beefy arms futile against the wood.

"Ah, here you are!" Aunty Agnes said, marching into the
kitchen like she'd caught criminals in the act.

Aunty Agnes opened the fridge and took out a bottle of
water. She filled a glass, proceeded to guzzle the water in
long, noisy gulps, and then returned the half-empty bottle to

the fridge. Buchi moved his stool away from the sink, closer to Aunty Ifueko. He watched her slide the blade of a knife down a plantain's skin with more force than was necessary. The skinned plantain was a pale yellow, with a line running down its length, marking the path of the knife. Aunty Ifueko put it in a bowl with other peeled plantains. Buchi stretched his neck to see beyond her body to the sink, where Aunty Agnes was squirting washing-up liquid into her palm. She turned on the tap. Buchi felt a sudden tingling on the back of his neck.

"Buchi," Aunty Agnes said. "Don't you greet your elders?"

More than any adult he knew, Aunty Agnes was very keen on demanding what she thought of as respect. If she walked into a room in the midst of chatter and laughter, she insisted on an immediate explanation, joining in only when she'd been fully briefed and was confident that she wasn't the target. Maybe she imagined that everyone talked about her because she wasn't married but had a son. Where the children were concerned, she got her respect with her sharp tone and the bullet-quick limbs she deployed every now and then to twist an ear or spank an errant bottom.

"Good afternoon, Aunty," Buchi murmured.

Aunty Agnes acknowledged the greeting with a grunt. "What are you doing in the kitchen when your mates are outside? Why not go and play with your sister and your cousin?"

"Yes, Aunty," Buchi said. He stepped off his stool and was shuffling toward the door when Aunty Ifueko's voice stopped him.

"Agnes, leave him, abeg," she said. "He's helping me. Buchi, stay."

Buchi hid his smile as he walked back to his stool.

"Okay o," Aunty Agnes said. "If you like, turn the boy into a woman wrapper."

"Haba, Agnes," Aunty Ifueko said, "there's nothing wrong with Buchi learning his way around a kitchen. It's a good thing for any child, boy or girl."

The kitchen was quiet for a moment. "Ah, sorry o," Aunty Agnes said. "I didn't know you're the expert on children."

Buchi heard Aunty Ifueko catch her breath as Aunty Agnes left the kitchen. He saw the knife tremble in her hand, and he inched close to the edge of the stool until his arm met the warmth of her hip.

Aunty Ifueko's childlessness was only ever mentioned in whispers. "So sad," his mother would say, while Aunty Agnes hinted at some unknown darkness in Aunty Ifueko's past. But Buchi knew there was no darkness in his Aunty Ifueko. She was good and gentle and kind, even to things. Like how whenever he showed her his sketch pad, she always held it delicately, flipping page after page without saying a word, sometimes smiling and other times frowning, but not in a bad way, more like she was trying to concentrate on a tiny detail. She always gave a decisive nod after she flipped past the last drawing. One time she said, "Wow, we have an artist in the family!" And in that moment Buchi knew that even though she often played football with Ogo in the backyard and praised Chinelo for how well she could spell, it was him, Buchi, that she liked best.

He hated that he couldn't fight Aunty Agnes on Aunty Ifueko's behalf—he was only eight—but he did what he thought her child would do to comfort her. He put his arms around her, carefully, in case she was in pain. She looked down at him. He saw her breathe out, felt the warm air on his face as she offered a shaky smile.

· · ·

BUCHI SAT OUTSIDE IN THE shade of the guava tree later that afternoon, Aunty Ifueko's plantain porridge still warm in his stomach. His pencil hovered over his sketch pad as he tried to ignore the noise from Chinelo and Ogo playing across from him, near the compound's walled fence. He erased a smudge from the page and decided the eyes he'd drawn were an accurate likeness of Aunty Agnes's bulbous ones. He considered giving her a snout. He could make her chin hairs curl up to the top of the page.

Buchi heard shrieking from Chinelo and squinted up from his pad. He nibbled on the end of his pencil and watched her, sunlight glinting off her dark skin. Her hair, plaited into four long braids that reached her shoulders, bounced and swayed with her every movement. They were playing ten-ten, stamping their feet and clapping, Chinelo bent forward at the waist. Chinelo won, of course, and, like the sour winner that she was, she did a victory dance around Ogo, shaking her hips and waving her fingers in his face while he tried to swat them away. Buchi had never understood ten-ten. He knew it had something to do with timing and the foot that each person played, but every time Chinelo tried to explain it to him, he got even more confused. "Let's just play," she'd say. "You'll understand it when you play." And then she would win and do her stupid dances. Even when they played simpler games like hide-and-seek, Chinelo always won. She was a cheater. He was sure of this even though he'd never caught her. There was no other explanation for her unending winning streak. At some point he'd started turning down all of Chinelo's invitations to play.

There was a time, not too long ago, when he and Chinelo had felt closer. Back when their parents used to fight. Their mother would yell at their father about his too-young, too-curvy assistant, how miserable she was at home all day, how much he and his children had taken from her. Chinelo would appear at Buchi's door with books tucked under her arm. While their mother's screams shook the walls, Buchi drew and Chinelo read out loud from Enid Blyton, softly conjuring images of blond children and tea parties. They would pretend not to hear slammed doors and the roar of their father's car as he fled the house. Then something changed without warning. The nights began to pass in silence. Their mother grew vacantly calm, drifting through the house on feet made of clouds. Buchi wondered if their mother's new headache pills had anything to do with this development; they looked nothing like the large round Panadol tablets he and Chinelo were given for aches.

All of that felt like years ago. Now, the only time some of the tension seemed to creep back into their mother's bones was around Christmas when she prepared to host their father's family. And Chinelo, she didn't need him anymore; she had plenty of friends at school, unlike Buchi. Since his one friend, Otolorin, moved to Abuja with his family, he'd found no replacements, overly suspicious when other kids at school tried to talk to him outside of the usual borrowing a pencil or other mundane class interaction. Was he being invited to play ball because they liked him, or just to make up the numbers, or so he could be the scapegoat when his team lost? He'd stay contemplating the question, paralyzed for so long that the other kids assumed a no and moved on. It made sense, then, that invitations to birthday parties often arrived addressed to "Chinelo Okezie" in careful childlike handwriting, the words "and Buchi" scribbled in different ink, like an afterthought.

"Ugh, this game is for girls," Ogo said, planting his hands on his hips. "I want to play something else."

"You're just saying that because I won," Chinelo said.

Buchi imagined Chinelo and Ogo's standoff escalating, lasers shooting out of their eyes—red from Chinelo's and blue from Ogo's—each turning the other into a stone statue. Buchi chuckled, and at that very moment Chinelo turned her gaze to the guava tree that Buchi was sitting beneath. And even though Buchi knew she could not have heard his quiet laughter from that distance, he regretted it.

"You want to climb the guava tree?" Chinelo asked Ogo.

Ogo seemed to consider this; then he whirled and headed for the tree. Chinelo rushed forward so she could lead, and she and Ogo ended up racing each other, Chinelo winning. She smirked at Ogo as she struggled to catch her breath. Buchi pretended to be absorbed with his sketch pad.

"Watch," Chinelo said, hiking her skirt up above her knees in preparation. "I'm going to reach the highest branch." She stepped closer to the tree. Buchi could see her bare feet on the ground beside his thighs. She nudged him with a foot. "Buchi, move."

"Go away," Buchi muttered without looking at her.

"We want to climb the tree," Chinelo said.

"You're not allowed to climb the tree, Mummy said so," Buchi said.

"*Nye nye nye nye nye nye nye*, Mummy said so," Chinelo said, jerking her head back and forth like a clucking hen while Ogo laughed. Buchi stayed put, his pencil now moving blindly over the surface of his pad. His stomach felt tight. If he just ignored them, they would get bored and leave.

"You want to go and tell your mummy?" Ogo sneered.

"Ogo, just climb over him," Chinelo said.

"Oh . . . I thought you wanted to go first," Ogo said.

"No, you can go first," Chinelo said. When Ogo hesitated, she added, "Or are you scared of him?"

Ogo rolled his eyes. "Scared of what, his big head?"

Buchi felt the tightness in his stomach creep up to his chest as Ogo leaned over his head to grab the tree trunk. Then he made to hoist himself onto Buchi's knee, knocking Buchi's sketch pad to the ground.

Buchi shoved Ogo hard in the stomach, and Ogo lost his balance. He fell, his head hitting the ground with a dull thud.

"Mummy, Mummy, Buchi has killed Ogo!" Chinelo screamed, running toward the house. She had barely made it to the front door when the adults started spilling out. Buchi's mother, Aunty Agnes, and Aunty Ifueko surrounded the wailing Ogo.

"What happened to my baby?" Aunty Agnes said.

Buchi's heart was hammering in his chest. His fingers and toes tingled.

Aunty Agnes followed Chinelo's pointing finger to Buchi. "Buchi!"

"Agnes, calm down," Aunty Ifueko said. "Let's take Ogo inside first."

Aunty Ifueko attempted to lift Ogo from the ground, but Aunty Agnes swatted her hands away. She gave Buchi a lingering glare before scooping her son into her arms and heading for the house, Aunty Ifueko trailing a few paces behind her.

. . .

THAT EVENING, AUNTY IFUEKO poked her head into Buchi's room, where his mother had put him in isolation. Buchi knew he wasn't allowed to have company while he was being punished, but he would not tell. Aunty Ifueko stepped into the room, shutting the door gently behind her. She sat beside him on his bed.

Aunty Ifueko didn't come into his room very often, and so now he looked around, trying to see the space through her eyes.

His desk wasn't as tidy as he'd have liked. He had some comic books strewn on it, a few coloring pencils and loose paper. But his clothes were put away, folded in his dresser, and his toys were in their bins.

"Buchi, what happened? You fought your cousin?"

"I didn't fight him," Buchi said, alarmed. He didn't want her thinking he was bad. "He was trying to climb me like a tree, so I pushed him away."

Aunty Ifueko nodded. "I believe you," she said. "Ogo is just a troublemaker like his mo—"

Aunty Ifueko stopped, her mouth hanging open in a small O. Then her lips curved into a smile and she laughed. Buchi laughed too.

Buchi often wondered what would happen if he offered himself to Aunty Ifueko, to be her child. He would go live with her, and after a few months his family would forget he'd ever been with them. And he would play along. This room would gather cobwebs in his absence, and when he saw Godwin and Gloria Okezie at Christmas, he would call them Uncle and Aunty, and his sister would be Cousin Chinelo. He'd complain about the dry Christmases in Nigeria, with the harmattan wind scouring his lips and the inside of his throat. With time he would start to speak a little differently, like Aunty Ifueko, who said *candy* instead of *sweets* and *cookies* instead of *biscuits*. Like her, he too would laugh and say, "I've lived in America too long."

"Aunty."

"Hmm?"

"Can I come and live with you in America?"

"Live with me?" Aunty Ifueko frowned. "Oh, you mean visit? Well, yes, of course. I'm sure we can arrange something. I'll have to ask your parents . . ."

Buchi looked away. He tried to name the thing he was feeling. Annoyed. For the first time, he was annoyed with Aunty Ifueko. Was she just as bad at listening as any other adult? But then she smiled at him, and he allowed his annoyance to fade. So it would be just a visit; that could be a first step. He would go next summer when school closed for long vacation. Who knew, maybe once he was there with her in New Jersey, a miracle would happen.

II

. . . .

IT WAS THE NEXT DECEMBER. BUCHI WAS READING A COMIC book in bed when he heard the front gate of the house open. He leapt from his bed to the window, where he had a view of the grounds below. A taxi stopped in front of the house and Uncle Michael rushed out of the back to the other side, where the door was already swinging open. He opened it the rest of the way and helped Aunty Ifueko out of the vehicle. Aunty Ifueko's smile was so wide, it looked like the wrong size, too big for her face. She was wearing her hair in long multicolored braids, pulled back in a ponytail as if to put the new roundness of her cheeks on display. If Buchi hadn't already known Aunty Ifueko was pregnant, he would have assumed she'd just gained some weight.

After his mother shared the news of Aunty Ifueko's pregnancy in September, Buchi had tried for a long time to be happy for his aunty. He told himself this was good. Aunty Ifueko would no longer have that sad look she sometimes got when she thought nobody was watching. Aunty Agnes's words would not have the power to cut her anymore. But he'd always thought of himself and Aunty Ifueko as outsiders together, two people who didn't quite belong in the family, who needed and were there for each other. With a baby, she wouldn't need him anymore. It had begun happening already, this pulling apart. How else could he explain why the visit Aunty Ifueko promised last December hadn't happened this past summer like they'd agreed?

Now Aunty Ifueko was walking toward the front door, his mother and Aunty Agnes hurrying to embrace her. They led her into the house, smiling, cradling her like she was suddenly a precious thing. Buchi decided he would not hurry down to greet her like he always did. In fact, he would avoid her the whole time she was here, to pay her back for the visit that hadn't happened. And if indeed she was still the same Aunty Ifueko, if he was still special to her, she would look for him.

And so Buchi distanced himself from Aunty Ifueko. He stopped seeking her out each time her voice or scent wafted into a room. He went the opposite direction if their paths were about to cross. When the family ate together, he refused to look at her; if she spoke to him, he directed his responses at his plate. He resented the fullness of her cheeks, the glimmer in her eyes. He sat in his room, anticipating the door swinging open and Aunty Ifueko poking her head through. He imagined that he would try not to smile, that he would wear his grudge snugly. But with each day that passed without her coming to find him, Buchi's heart sank further into his stomach. He wondered if Aunty Ifueko would ever notice that her shadow was no longer attached to her, that it had come undone and was skulking around the house like a dark cloud.

One afternoon, there was a knock on his bedroom door, and Aunty Ifueko appeared.

"Buchi, have you been avoiding me?" she said.

Buchi didn't know which feeling inside him was stronger, gladness that she'd finally come, resentment that it had taken her so long, or annoyance at the slightly amused tone of her voice.

He didn't look up from his Brick Game, but Tetris shapes cascaded down the screen without his guidance, forming an ugly tower.

"Can I come in?"

Buchi nodded and Aunty Ifueko walked in. The fabric of her flowing boubou was printed with little owls in bright colors. She wasn't yet doing that duck waddle that pregnant women did, but he could see the slight protrusion of her stomach, like she was hiding a small round package under her clothes. She sat next to him on his bed.

"I've been asking everybody, where's my little helper, where's my shadow? Don't you want to help me wrap gifts?"

Buchi said nothing.

"I know you're disappointed about not coming to visit this summer," Aunty Ifueko said. "Things got so busy at work; I knew I wouldn't have been able to take time off. I'm sorry, oh?"

She allowed the silence to sit for a while. Then, "Can I have a hug?"

Buchi shrugged, but he was smiling on the inside. Aunty Ifueko wrapped her arms around him, enclosing him in owl-patterned fabric, and he let his Brick Game slip from his fingers onto his bed. He was surprised at the firmness of Aunty Ifueko's stomach pressing against him. He'd thought babies were supposed to be squishy, fragile things, but Aunty Ifueko's tummy was hard like a wall. It didn't matter, though. She had come looking for him, to apologize. So what if she was having a baby.

"Ah, that's better," Aunty Ifueko sighed. She released him from her embrace. "I really wanted you and Chinelo to come; I even talked to your mum about it. But the timing just wasn't good this year."

Buchi stared at Aunty Ifueko's face, her voice fading out of his hearing. He watched her fail to realize the effect her words were having on him. His visit with her would have included Chinelo? A salty taste flooded his mouth. If he wasn't special enough to deserve a visit with Aunty Ifueko, just him by himself, when there was no baby, how much worse would things get with a baby around?

Aunty Ifueko stood to leave. "So are you coming to help me with the gifts? Now that I've been forgiven?"

Buchi reached for his Brick Game with a shaky hand. "Sorry, Aunty. I'm tired."

. . .

THE FAMILY WAS SETTLING AROUND the dining table when Buchi went down for dinner. The massive table was crowded with platters of steaming jollof rice and fried meats, plantains, pounded yam, egusi, and pepper soup. The room was buzzing with good cheer—even Aunty Agnes was able to let go of her perpetual scowl. Aunty Ifueko was quiet throughout the meal. But it wasn't a sad quiet. It was the kind of quiet that was filled with something. She had gone and made a new person, an accomplice, without him. Buchi's insides churned. He wanted to hurl his plate at the nearest wall.

Back in his room, Buchi flipped through the sketches he'd done that afternoon after he spoke with Aunty Ifueko: collages of babies with tails and hydra heads and incisors and tentacles and stingers, pages and pages of them. He imagined their cartoon villain laughter as they mocked him. He ripped the pages out one by one, then soaked them in his bathroom sink and watched them go soft. He made the paper into pulp, and he squeezed and squeezed like pulp was a thing that could die.

III

A YEAR HAD PASSED, AND SOME THINGS, IT SEEMED, would never be the same. And Buchi was fine with that. On the day that family was due to begin arriving at their house, their mother called Buchi and Chinelo together. "I want you two to be careful around Aunty Ifueko," she said. "Be very nice to her, okay? Don't bother her. She's . . . not feeling very well."

"Is she sick?" Chinelo asked.

"Not exactly," their mother said.

Buchi mumbled something to indicate that he understood, even though he wasn't sure he did. Either way, he didn't intend to have anything to do with Aunty Ifueko or her baby.

At dinner that night, Buchi had little appetite for the beans and fried plantains. His mother seemed subdued. Even Ogo, who had arrived that evening with his mother, was on his best behavior.

"Michael confirmed he and Ifueko are arriving on the twenty-third," Buchi's father said.

"I thought they might change their minds about coming this year," Buchi's mother said. "That would have been understandable, with everything that's happened."

"It's good for them to come," Aunty Agnes said. "It'll help to take Ifueko's mind off things." Buchi was confused. But before he could ask what things Aunty Ifueko would want to take her mind off, Aunty Agnes continued, "Michael is a good man. Ifueko has nothing to worry about. Some other men would have taken another wife a long time ago or gotten one small girl pregnant from God knows where. Thirteen years they've been trying. Ifueko is lucky she married into a good family."

"Hmm," Buchi's mother said with a stiff smile.

Aunty Agnes went on. "And they can always try again. Ifueko isn't too old."

Buchi's confusion grew. But it was Chinelo who asked the question.

"Did something happen to Aunty Ifueko's baby?"

Only then did things start to add up in Buchi's head, like his mother urging him and Chinelo to give Aunty Ifueko space.

Aunty Agnes turned to Buchi's mother. "Gloria, you didn't tell them?"

Buchi's mother fiddled with her cutlery. Buchi's father shook his head. The look on his face was the same as when Buchi fell short. Buchi hadn't known his mother could also be subjected to that look.

"Aunty Ifueko lost the baby," Aunty Agnes said.

Buchi's fingers turned to jelly. His spoon clattered onto his plate.

"You mean . . . the baby died?" Chinelo said.

Aunty Agnes nodded.

Chinelo burst into tears, and their mother and Aunty Agnes rushed to her side. Buchi sat still, listening to Chinelo sob and the adults mumble vague comforts. He stood and muttered something about going to his room. But as he passed by his mother, she reached out and pulled him into the sandwich of bodies. He breathed in the warm, mingled breath, and in that cocoon he, too, began to cry.

Over the past year, Buchi had managed to push the thought of Aunty Ifueko's pregnancy out of his mind, pretend it didn't exist. At first, he was obsessed with sketching mutant babies: ugly babies with oversized heads and limbs, pincers and tentacles that could grab on or wrap around and never let go, babies with dark, suction-cup mouths that led into bottomless pits where no light could survive. He filled sketch pad after sketch pad with these images, and after each pad was filled, he tore the sheets off and soaked them in his bathroom sink, watching the water eat up the paper. And when the paper was soft and pliable, he would smush it into pulp and scoop it up into the toilet and flush. He felt better afterward. For a while. The ritual eventually lost its appeal as he came to terms with its futility. He told himself that the best thing he could do was ignore it, ignore Aunty Ifueko and her profound betrayal. He sketched other things: birds and lizards, his mother riding on a cloud, the one-eyed beggar at the roundabout on the way to school. He let Chinelo beat him at ten-ten.

But now, in the midst of his sadness for Aunty Ifueko, hope was blooming. A new chance. There was something almost magical about the moment—the possibility of something good rising out of a tragedy. This time he swore he wouldn't dawdle. When he saw Aunty Ifueko again, he would ask her to take him back to America with her. His parents would say yes, too touched by her pain and need to refuse. He wouldn't even have to pack; they'd get all new things. New things for a new life in New Jersey, with her. Soft and aching from her loss, she would be ever so grateful to him for coming to her rescue. She would realize that he was better than a million babies.

. . .

TWO DAYS BEFORE CHRISTMAS, Aunty Ifueko arrived with Uncle Michael. Buchi ran out to greet her but stopped short when he saw Chinelo and Ogo surrounding Aunty Ifueko already. When Aunty Ifueko was freed from their hugs, she reached into her large bag and dispensed packets of sweets, and Chinelo and Ogo scampered off.

Without the bodies of the children covering Aunty Ifueko, Buchi noticed how her dress swallowed her. The skin of her face was slack, like a balloon that was losing its air. Still, he took comfort in the sameness of the routine: Aunty Ifueko arriving, always bearing gifts for the naughty and the nice, the children gathering around her, tugging at her clothes until they were appeased by her offering.

Buchi was stepping forward to hug Aunty Ifueko when his mother and Aunty Agnes hurried out of the house. They surrounded Aunty Ifueko and steered her inside, past where Buchi stood alone.

. . .

THE AIR AROUND THE LUNCH TABLE on Christmas Eve was stilted, as if there were sullen ghosts floating about the room, sucking out any traces of joy or cheer. Aunty Agnes, after several attempts at starting a conversation, had given up and sat chewing her food like she held it responsible for the silence.

Buchi hadn't had a chance yet to be alone with Aunty Ifueko, to say all the things he wanted to say. As soon as she'd arrived the day before, she'd disappeared into her room and he hadn't seen her until that morning at breakfast. He'd greeted her good morning and she'd answered with a smile, looking past him. After breakfast she'd returned to her room. Now Buchi watched as she forked rice into her mouth like she was performing a delicate art.

After lunch, everyone gathered in the living room for a movie. By some miracle, Chinelo and Ogo were able to quickly agree on *Toy Story 2*. As Buzz Lightyear flew through space in the opening scene, Buchi watched Aunty Ifueko's every move. A few minutes into the movie, she excused herself. He counted slowly to one hundred, and when she hadn't returned, he slipped out of the room. He went out to the quarters behind the house, and through the bedroom door, which was open just a crack, he found her lying in bed, her back to the entrance. The door creaked as he nudged it farther.

"Mike, don't start again," Aunty Ifueko sighed. "I told you I didn't want to come here."

Buchi stopped. It had never crossed his mind that Aunty Ifueko wouldn't want to come to Lagos, to their house. Even with everything that had happened with her baby, and even with Aunty Agnes's subtle hostilities over the years, he'd imagined that some part of Aunty Ifueko had always wanted to be there, for him at least. But now he found himself doubting, again. How many of these December gatherings had she ever really wanted to be present at? All these years, had he been yet another thing she'd had to endure?

Aunty Ifueko raised her torso and turned her neck just enough to look behind her at the door. She squinted at him.

"Oh, Buchi."

Buchi's smile was tentative, and he waited for her to give one of her own. But she laid her head back down on the pillow, turning away from him again.

"Why aren't you watching the movie with everyone else?" Aunty Ifueko asked, still not looking at him.

Buchi took a gamble and stepped forward. "I just came to check on you."

"I am fine, Buchi," she said, her voice like a fading song. "Just fine."

But Buchi knew better. The old Aunty Ifueko would have been in the living room letting Chinelo and Ogo compete for her attention, each one hurrying to predict every plot turn of the movie before it happened. "Fine" was when Aunty Ifueko laughed from deep within her stomach and called him "my shadow" like she meant it.

Just as Buchi took another step toward the bed, Aunty Ifueko's voice stopped him. "Please, shut the door when you leave," she said. Buchi stood there trying to decide whether she was asking him to go, or just reminding him to close the door when he did choose to leave.

When he'd first come to her door he'd had a plan for how he would start to make her well again. He would begin with a hug, to soothe the hurt. He would not tell her about drawing and flushing mutant babies; that would sound bad. Instead, he would say that there was no need for her to be sad anymore since he was there. He would say that they could go together and present a united front to his parents, ask them to let him go back to America with her, to help Aunty Ifueko recover, only for a while. And then a while would turn into months and months into years until he was absorbed into her life such that they could not be separated without drawing blood. Years would pass and everyone would forget that things had ever been different, and she would not be childless anymore because, like a miracle that happened when no one was looking, he would have become her son.

But now he was realizing a key flaw in his plan: Aunty Ifueko didn't want him, not as a son, not even as her shadow. And perhaps the version of Aunty Ifueko that he wanted—the one who was always happy to see him, whose bad feelings could be cured by a hug from him—had never really existed.

And even if this plan was somehow possible, him moving in permanently with Aunty Ifueko and pulling off this tacit adoption, time had a way of tugging at loose strings, turning new things old and stale. Days and weeks and months would pass, and there would be something else for Aunty Ifueko to want, something else for him to doubt, perhaps even something else to mourn.

Buchi shut the door behind him, nursing a sudden and quiet grief.

DEBRIS

●●●

D'BOY LURKED AROUND THE EDGE OF THE CROWD AT the newspaper vendor's stand, looking for a worthy pocket to pick. It was a good hunting spot. Most of the people gathered there had no intention of buying a paper, but that didn't stop them from reacting loudly to the headlines, their arguments sometimes leading to fistfights. D'boy scanned their back pockets, kicking a rusty can to avoid suspicion. Years of picking pockets had made his eyes discerning, his fingers nimble. But people had become warier too, men carrying valuables in their shirt pockets and women growing fonder of bags with short straps, so they could tuck the bags under their armpits.

D'boy decided that if his scrounging attempts at the vendor's proved unfruitful, he would proceed to the nearest bus stop. Fuel was scarce again in Lagos, and, with it, public transportation. The bus stops were packed with people wilting under the unrelenting sun, searching for the next danfo that would rattle to a stop so they could fight their way inside. D'boy imagined himself slipping into their midst as the chaos started. With multiple limbs clawing and shoving, his work would not be noticed until some unfortunate individuals managed to struggle onto a bus only to find their wallets gone when it was time to pay the fare. D'boy could not afford to spare them a thought. His stomach growled yet again, reminding him of rule number one: stomach before conscience.

A few years ago, D'boy had been introduced to his father, an enigma known to him merely as Spanner. He'd lived with his mother all his life, until that morning when, without warning, she'd taken him and his few belongings on a long bus ride. They arrived at a vast compound of bungalows with crumbling one-room apartments, and she left him in front of room seven. Her instructions were to ask for Spanner, and to tell him that he, D'boy, was his son by way of Tinuke. She'd left without a goodbye, and D'boy hadn't seen her since. After knocking for several minutes and getting no answer, he'd sat outside that door for hours, growing tired and hungry, ignored by the people who passed him. He'd learnt rule number one then: every man for himself.

Spanner had come home that night long after the compound had gone to sleep. D'boy lay curled up in front of the door, on the corridor that would turn out to be his bed many nights. He was prodded awake by a foot. Spanner, with a gravelly voice, asked who he was. D'boy blinked up at Spanner, his eyes losing the weight of sleep, and recited his mother's message. The big, dark man examined D'boy in the light of the bulb overhead like he would a worthless, albeit fascinating, piece of debris that had washed up on his own private stretch of beach. He finally shoved his hand into the pocket of his trousers and dug out his key. Then he reached over D'boy's head to open the door to the room and, with a grunt, gestured for D'boy to go in. The room was dank and airless, with a mattress, a wardrobe, and little else.

D'boy had no fantasies of Spanner as the dutiful father. While his mother had bemoaned her fate every day she'd been saddled with him, Spanner simply ignored him. D'boy followed Spanner's lead, and in no time they managed to wordlessly carve out their separate islands in the small room, learning to meander around each other with minimal contact. As the weeks passed, D'boy learned nothing about his supposed father, except that he went away often for some kind of work. During these absences, which were sometimes long and always unannounced, D'boy would make his bed on the corridor, like he had that first day. Spanner hadn't thought to give him a key. D'boy hadn't thought to ask.

D'boy felt a gust of wind and glanced up in time to see Orobo—round and squashed-looking, as though some malignant force had pressed his body down into itself—whizzing past. Whenever he ran, which he did with a speed and ease that belied his bulk, it was for good reason. D'boy remembered the day when a riot broke out after a clash between police officers and okada drivers. He'd followed Orobo to safety then, and so now he spun and ran after him.

"Orobo, wetin dey happen?" D'boy asked.

"Food . . . food . . ."

That was all Orobo could manage. It was enough.

D'boy ran with Orobo all the way to the local primary school, through the gates and onto the school's football field, and there D'boy lost sight of him. In the center of the field there was a long table. On one side of it, four women stood handing out food in sealed foil packs, and on the other side were four untidy lines of children reaching almost to the school gates. As happened every once in a while, some organization was giving out food. When people talked about this kind of food, they called it "free." But those people were not sharp. They didn't know life's number one rule: nothing is ever free. In this case, though, the price was an easy one to pay. In exchange for full stomachs, pictures would be taken of the fed, mouths shiny with gratitude and oil from jollof rice.

D'boy noticed, beside a block of classrooms and half hidden among a cluster of banana trees, a few adults creeping around with sacks, into which some children were dropping their uneaten packs of food before rushing back to queue up for more. There were no adults on the queues; it looked like only children were getting fed this time. D'boy didn't feel like a child, and he didn't know if, technically, he was one. Like Orobo and many of the boys D'boy hung around with, D'boy didn't know his age and had never marked a birthday. Birthdays, like eyeglasses, were one of those things that only rich children seemed to need.

D'boy would get his meal pack, but not from joining the end of one of those queues, which were growing longer with every second. He had to make his way to the front. He positioned himself in a space between two lines of noisy children and snuck toward the table, avoiding the harried-looking young men brandishing bamboo sticks and trying to maintain order. He could see the tubs from which the packs of food were being given out. They were almost three-quarters empty, and the food was disappearing quickly. One of the women handing out the packs wiped sweat from her upper lip and beckoned to a man standing by a van parked nearby. D'boy knew what it meant: more food was needed, fast. The man shook his head and made a waving motion with both hands. D'boy also knew what that meant, and he was seized with panic. He dropped to his hands and knees and crept forward, making his way toward the tubs. Just as he stretched out his hand to grab a pack of food, his ankle was caught in a firm grip and he was yanked out from under the table.

"What are you doing there?" It was one of the men with sticks. "My friend, go stand for line before I break your head!"

D'boy scrambled to his feet and ran toward the end of the lines. But, knowing that if he joined a queue the food would be gone long before he reached the table, D'boy decided there was only one thing to do. Reaching the end of the queue, he took a deep breath and shot forward like a striking fist. As he gathered speed, he opened his mouth and let out a scream. The other children, seeing D'boy as he flew past and realizing what he was doing, broke rank. The lines collapsed into a stampede behind D'boy as he charged, the children's voices joining with his in a frightful roar. He'd never felt so hungry, so powerful.

Mere feet away from the table, his army raging behind him, D'boy saw one of the serving women look up at the advancing mob. She alerted the other women with a scream. The women let go of the food packs in their hands and fled for the safety of their van, where even the stick-wielding order keepers had gathered to watch with their arms folded as the wave of bodies surged.

It was called survival. That was rule number one.

LONG HAIR

∙∙∙

WHEN JENNIFER FIRST JOINED OUR SCHOOL, SHE DIDN'T know anything. She didn't know which wells had clear water for bathing, or that if you wanted fresh puffin bread you had to rush to the tuckshop once the bell rang for break. She was always late to the dining hall, so she got the smallest portions. I wondered which school she had transferred from, and whether the students there were all slow like her. She didn't have any friends—until the day she loosened her hair, which she'd been wearing plaited all-back, for the first time.

It was during siesta on a Saturday, and everyone was supposed to be on their beds reading or sleeping or crying quietly from homesickness. But the girls gathered around Jennifer that afternoon, even the dorm prefect, who should have sent them back to their beds. They were all saying how pretty she was. Me, I didn't think Jennifer was that pretty just because she had light skin and long, relaxer-straightened hair that reached the middle of her back. I stared at her hair as it came loose from the plaits and fell down her shoulders. She ran her fingers through it, from scalp to tip. It looked so shiny and soft. I wanted to go to her bed, reach out and touch it, like the other girls were doing. I remembered how my mother cut my hair short after I got my admission letter to this school, saying it was so I would focus on my books and not be distracted with caring for my hair. I told Dumebi, who slept on the bunk beside mine, that my hair used to be even longer than Jennifer's before my mother cut it. She only said *mhm*, the way people do when they know you're talking rubbish.

So that was how everybody became Jennifer's friend. All the girls in our year followed her everywhere, fighting among themselves for her attention. Even senior students treated her like an egg. They no longer sent her on errands, and during sanitation on Saturday mornings, the prefects gave her the easiest tasks; while some of us were cutting grass and scrubbing latrines, she was busy wiping windowpanes. All the seniors in our room claimed her as their school daughter, and they let her sit with them when they were gisting. People asked her all the time, *Jennifer, are you mixed? Jennifer, is your mother from London or America?* Jennifer liked it when the other girls asked her these silly questions; you could tell she was the proud type. We had all seen her parents, who were both fair like her but were Igbo, not white. Still, she would laugh and say yes to everything: *Yes, I am mixed. Yes, my mother is related to the queen of England.*

It wasn't as if I was the most popular girl in school or in my year before Jennifer came. Someone like me, I don't need so-called friends surrounding me all the time like flies on a dead rat. There are girls in my class that I walk to the library with, and sometimes I share my snacks with Dumebi. But after Amara and co. threw me out of their group last year just because I told Phidelia what Amara had been saying behind her back, that Phidelia had let all the boys in her neighborhood play with her breasts and this was why Phidelia was already wearing a D-cup bra when some of us were still begging our breasts to form—and Phidelia with her leaky mouth mentioned my name when confronting Amara—I learned that girls and their cliques can be very stupid.

Even though all the girls now liked Jennifer, I kept looking at her with side-eye; her type of hair needed an explanation. The girls I know don't have this kind of long hair just like that and for no reason. We pay for her type of hair at the market, and then we pay more at the salon so they can fix it in for us with thread or glue. Then we wear the hair for at least six weeks so the money we spent doesn't feel wasted. And when it starts to itch, we beat on our heads like drums, or we find something thin and firm to scratch with, because everyone knows your fingers can't reach your scalp when you have all that hair taking up space.

It pained me the way Jennifer started walking about the whole school like it was her father's compound. Everyone knew her. If a teacher sent you to go and call Jennifer and you asked which of the Jennifers, they would say the long-hair Jennifer, or the oyibo Jennifer. Every time I heard this, I wanted to pinch their lips shut the way my mother does when I say something stupid. Why was everybody always talking about her? Had they never seen a light-skinned person? And what a show-off Jennifer was! On weekdays, all the girls had to plait their hair in the style approved by the health prefect, except for those like me with low-cut hair. But on weekends, when there were no hairstyle rules, Jennifer would loosen her plaits, comb out her hair, and leave it free. You could easily point her out from afar because she would be the one who looked like she was wearing a large dark blanket on her head. All the girls kept saying, *Jennifer, come, let us touch your hair,* and with a sigh and a frown she would let them. She would keep the fake frown on her face as they played with her hair, twisting and untwisting it around their fingers, stretching it to see if they could make it reach her buttocks, saying, *Jennifer, you are so lucky, we wish we had hair like yours.* And Jennifer would sigh again and complain about how much shampoo and conditioner she had to use to care for her long hair. And the relaxer! Did they know she had to buy two big-size containers every time she needed to relax her hair? *Don't envy me*, she would say, stroking her hair like it was a living thing.

. . .

JENNIFER'S TROUBLES STARTED WHEN THIS one girl had a dream. Everyone called this girl Vision—or Senior Vision if, like me, they were in a class below her—because she could see the future in her dreams. One time she dreamt that there was heavy rain and the principal's house collapsed, killing him and his whole family. She said it would happen in three weeks. Many months passed, yet the principal's house remained standing. Another time she dreamt that a snake bit a student and she died. And truly, about a week later, some girls were cutting the tall elephant grass near the school's fence and they found a big snake. Senior Vision said it was only by the mercy of God that nobody died that day.

Anyway, Senior Vision had this dream. She said she saw a Mami Wota sitting at the bottom of the Atlantic Ocean with all her pretty girl servants. (All Mami Wota girls are fine; everybody knows this.) The Mami Wota said that she had sent one of her girls as an agent to our school, to make trouble. Senior Vision had a sweet mouth, and she knew how to tell stories. So when she started talking like this you believed her, even if you remembered that the principal's house was still standing.

The same day Senior Vision told her dream, it spread throughout the whole school. After that, when any little thing happened, everyone blamed the Mami Wota girl. It was the Mami Wota girl that went about stealing provisions and bathwater and pooing in classrooms. It was this demon in disguise who stood outside the dorms at night, tormenting innocent girls on their way to the latrines.

Then Senior Vision had another dream and announced that the Mami Wota girl was on a mission of death and anyone could be the target. We all had to be careful, she said, and sleep with one eye open, because the person you called your best friend, your bunkmate, your classmate, that could be the demon girl, and you could be the one she was sent to kill so you wouldn't fulfill your destiny. Everybody was shaking like wet birds in harmattan. We stopped walking alone after dark. More students were bed-wetting, and they blamed it on the Mami Wota girl. And it was true, in a way. Was it not fear of the demon that made girls lie on their beds and pee with their eyes wide open instead of going out to the latrines after lights out? I know because it happened to me once. Just once—I'm not a bed-wetter, and that story is not important.

But even though the school was upside down with this Mami Wota business, Jennifer just went about as if nothing bothered her. Like she wasn't one of us. So one morning, I whispered to Dumebi that Jennifer had been talking and laughing in her sleep the night before, that maybe she was talking to her fellow Mami Wota girls. I wasn't doing anything bad; I only said what I was thinking. Is it my fault that Dumebi carried the matter on her head and started asking some of the other girls in our dorm what they thought? They weren't sure if Mami Wota girls talked to each other in their sleep, they said, but it sounded like something that should be true. Plus, someone added, all demon girls were pretty, with light skin and long hair like Jennifer's. We all nodded—we had watched *Karishika*.

By evening the entire dorm was bubbling. Girls were whispering and pointing fingers and looking at each other in code. The demon was Jennifer and there was proof: one, her long hair; two, her fair skin and fine face; three, she spoke to her Mami Wota friends every night; four, she was such a deep sleeper that it took forever to wake her up, meaning her spirit traveled whenever she slept. One of the girls even said that Jennifer's name was a sign, when you added everything else: *Jennifer* rhymed with *Lucifer*, and Lucifer was the father of all evil.

I didn't feel sorry for Jennifer. She was busy pretending not to notice that the girls were not talking to her anymore, that nobody called her to admire her hair, or asked her to walk with them to the shops, or begged her for cubes of sugar. As the days went on, I noticed that her followers started finding ways to avoid her, to show everybody that no o, they really weren't that close. But Jennifer kept acting normal. I whispered to Dumebi that this was what a proper Mami Wota girl would do, act normal while everyone else ran mad.

The next day, when we gathered outside the dorms for evening prayers, someone kept mentioning Jennifer's name in their prayer, asking God for protection from evil. I did not see what happened next because I was focused on my own prayers, but I heard later that Jennifer jumped on the girl and that was how the fight started. We formed a circle around them as Jennifer held the girl's body to the ground and plastered her face with slaps. Jennifer was screaming, *Shut up shut up*, and the girl was trying hard to hit Jennifer's face. But Jennifer was an expert. The way she lifted her neck and face up out of reach while using her knees and one hand to pin the girl down, you would know she had fought many battles before, maybe even in the spirit world. It took two prefects and the matron to separate Jennifer from the poor girl.

The other girls whispered evidence number five among themselves: Jennifer clearly had supernatural strength, dark powers from the depths of hell.

It was only after they pulled Jennifer away that I noticed the other girl was Dumebi. The matron dragged Jennifer and Dumebi to her house, and they did not return to the dorm until long after lights out. I know because I stayed awake waiting for Dumebi. I asked her what had happened with the matron, but she just turned her back to me and covered herself with her wrapper. As if it was me who'd asked her to go and fight Jennifer. I turned my back too and went to sleep.

The next day, Jennifer and Dumebi were sent to work with the kitchen staff as punishment. When they returned to the room in the evening, everyone went quiet as if they were expecting something to happen. But Jennifer went to her corner and Dumebi went to hers, and slowly the others went back to their business.

. . .

DUMEBI KEPT ACTING FUNNY the rest of the week. She seemed angry and wouldn't speak to anyone, not even me. I think she was expecting us to thank her for fighting Jennifer, even though she had lost. In a way, Jennifer had lost also, because everyone was even more afraid of her now.

Late one Saturday night, when we were all asleep, Dumebi crept to Jennifer's bed with a pair of scissors and started cutting off her hair. She had gone about halfway when Jennifer woke up screaming, waking the whole room. Somebody turned on the lights, and we all stared from our beds with our mouths wide open. Dumebi was standing bent over Jennifer's bed, holding the scissors in her right hand and a fistful of hair in her left. Clumps of dark hair were scattered across Jennifer's pillow and had spilled onto the floor.

Jennifer sat up in her lower bunk bed and touched the bare half of her head with shaky fingers. She looked like a lost child, and for a moment I felt sorry for her. But then she flew from her bed, screaming like the demon she was, and attacked Dumebi. She pushed Dumebi to the floor and sat on her stomach. She grabbed handfuls of Dumebi's hair, but it was not long enough for her to get a good grip, so she started slapping and punching. By this time, the entire dorm was in chaos; some girls were banging on their lockers and cheering, others were running from the room, but nobody dared to get in Jennifer's way. Dumebi managed to reach up and scratch Jennifer across her left eyelid. Jennifer froze. She touched the scratch and then stared at the red stain on her finger like she'd never known the color of her own blood.

Seeing her chance at freedom, Dumebi shoved Jennifer, who fell to the side, just within reach of the pair of scissors Dumebi had been holding at the start of the fight. Dumebi crawled away, but before she could get far, Jennifer reached for the scissors and thrust the sharp end into the back of Dumebi's thigh. Blood poured from the wound, down Dumebi's leg and onto the floor. Dumebi stayed on her hands and knees and cried for her mummy, and Jennifer just cried. She let the scissors fall to the floor and wiped her hands over and over on her nightdress.

· · ·

THEY SENT JENNIFER AND DUMEBI home on an indefinite suspension, after the principal paraded Jennifer before the whole school during morning assembly—they could not display Dumebi because of her injury. The principal called them a pair of bad eggs. Jennifer wore what was left of her hair swept to one side of her head, to cover the shorn half, but the breeze wouldn't stop blowing it around. She stared at a spot above our heads as she stood in front of us. The principal said there was no guarantee that Jennifer and Dumebi would be allowed back; there would be a disciplinary panel to decide.

Dumebi never came back; her parents withdrew her from our school. But now, three weeks after the incident, Jennifer has returned. Her hair is cut short, like mine, and Senior Vision has had new dreams that have nothing to do with Jennifer. Still, nobody talks to her. I see her all the time, walking by herself with her face to the ground like she dropped something. Sometimes, part of me wants to feel bad for her. But, honestly, I think I like this new Jennifer. I imagine going to her and asking to borrow her bucket or her English textbook, and staying a moment too long so she has someone to talk to.

One day, she was standing in front of me in the dining hall queue. I tapped her on the shoulder, and when she turned around, I told her that I liked her low cut, that it fit her face better than the long hair that had made everybody go mad. She frowned and turned away, but I knew she was happy that somebody had talked to her.

Jennifer might not agree, but I know that everything that happened was for her own good, so she could learn that nobody is special. Maybe we can even be friends, now that she has become humble.

ANIMALS

· ·

NEDU NAMED THE CHICKEN OTUANYA BECAUSE IT WAS MISS-
ing an eye, a film of pink tissue sealing the space where the organ
should have been. He summoned his father, older sister, Cherish,
and unsmiling mother to the backyard for a naming ceremony,
where he served peanuts and Fanta and solemnly announced the
chicken's name to polite applause from his father and an eye roll
from his sister. After his family dispersed, Nedu lingered in the
backyard. He fed Otuanya leftover grains of rice and tickled the
fleshy red wattles that dangled under the chicken's beak.

The chicken had come into their lives two evenings ago,
crouched on the floor in the back of his mother's car. Nedu and
his sister watched her open the rear door of the car as wide as
it would go. She bent toward the chicken. It gave a warning
cluck and she straightened up, wiping her palms on the front
of her skirt. Nedu frowned. He'd never seen his mother afraid
of anything. Not too long ago, she'd gotten their whole family
dragged to the police station after she called an officer and his
future generations useless and unfortunate. In the days following
that incident, Nedu had hoped someone would bring it up—
maybe his dad would make a joke to open the conversation, or
his mother would cite yet another news story about the police.
Maybe then, inside the nest of their words, he could confess

that since that day, each time he saw the impenetrable black of a police uniform, his heart threw itself against the walls of his chest. Was it just him? That afternoon at the station, his eyes had fixated on one officer's weapon: a dull AK-47 with a rash of rust creeping across the barrel like an infection. He'd seen police guns before, but never that close. The way the gun hung by a dirty strap from the officer's shoulder, with the ease and innocence of an old backpack. The light-headed dread that had him blindly groping for Cherish, to hide his shaking hand in hers.

"Mum, should I google how to carry a chicken?" Cherish asked, a hint of amusement in her voice, her phone materializing.

Their mother, Uzoma, waved a dismissive hand. She ducked again into the back of the car and reemerged clutching the squawking chicken by the wings. The chicken's legs were bound with a length of string, claws scratching at air. Uzoma hurried around the side of the house to the backyard. Nedu and Cherish followed, Cherish brandishing her phone, camera ready, in the hopes of capturing some social-media-worthy shenanigan. In the backyard, their mother undid the string binding the chicken's legs together and tied one leg to a clothesline pole. Nedu stared at the chicken in the fading evening light. That was when he first noticed the missing eye. Nedu had once had a boil on his left eyelid so big that he couldn't open it for days. His heart went out to the bird.

When their father returned from work that evening, Cherish told him about the chicken in the backyard. He seemed pleased. "You can always taste the difference between the frozen kind and the ones that are cooked fresh," he said. Then, to his wife, "But, Uzoma, I didn't know you could kill a chicken o." He smirked at Nedu and Cherish. "You see this my wife of secret talents?"

"Lol," Cherish said. "Mummy the chicken slayer."

Nedu knew, of course, that his mother hadn't bought the chicken as a pet. His parents had made their no-pets policy clear the day he cried himself sick begging to adopt a puppy from his friend's dog's litter. Besides, nobody kept chickens as pets. But he lay in bed that night thinking about the chicken, alone in the backyard. He wondered if having one eye made it easier to fall asleep. He crept out of bed to watch the bird from his window, a dark shape barely visible under the blanket of night. That was when the idea for the naming ceremony came to him. It made sense: if you gave a thing a name, you couldn't turn around and eat it as food. And so after Nedu performed the ceremony, and the third and fourth and fifth days of Otuanya's life passed uninterrupted, he let his heart settle.

The chicken became the best part of Nedu's days. When he woke up, he would race from his room, down the stairs, and out to the backyard. He hung up his mother's old banana-print wrapper, tying its four corners to the clotheslines and creating a small canopy to protect Otuanya from the sun. He extended the tether that tied Otuanya's leg to the clothesline pole by using strips of cloth cut from an old dish towel. He took some of his toys out to the backyard and was disappointed when he couldn't get Otuanya to perch on his remote-controlled monster truck for a ride. Every time Nedu had to leave Otuanya—to make his bed, or for his mandatory study period supervised by Cherish, or to watch reruns of *Ben 10* in the cool of the air-conditioned living room— he felt guilty, worried that Otuanya would be lonely without him. The thought was almost enough to bring him to tears.

· · ·

AT FIRST, UZOMA WAS AMUSED by her son's fondness for the chicken and allowed him responsibility for its care. With school on break, she figured, the bird would keep the seven-year-old occupied. But, as the days passed, Uzoma became wary of her son's growing attachment to the animal. She began reminding him of Otuanya's ultimate destiny. Pulling her earlobes and adopting a singsong voice, she'd say, "Remember, remember, all roads lead to my pepper soup pot."

But it was now two weeks since she'd brought the chicken home, and even as Uzoma sung her reminders to Nedu, she was losing confidence in her ability to usher the bird to its savory fate. Ebube, her husband, had sounded so impressed that she'd bought a live chicken, and with each day that passed, it became harder to admit to him that she hadn't given prior thought to the logistics of the killing. The first week they'd had it, her husband had returned from work each evening sniffing his way to the kitchen, wide-eyed and hopeful. She'd made excuses all that week, her tone getting sharper each day, and was relieved when he stopped asking. But her relief soon turned to shame. This past week, she'd imagined the chicken taunting her each time she went to the backyard to set out the trash or bring in laundry from the clothesline. She considered returning to the market for precut chicken parts to make her soup with, but then her husband would know she was avoiding having to kill the chicken she'd bought on impulse.

She still wasn't sure why she'd bought a live chicken in the first place—she'd never killed one before. Maybe this was a new iteration of the strange unrest she'd been feeling for weeks, ever since that thing with the policeman. Or perhaps it was simply the curl of the chicken seller's lip when Uzoma had asked for the price on a whim. The woman had gestured toward her freezer full of chicken parts instead. "Fine madam like you," she said, "you go fit kill chicken?"

She would do it today, she decided, while it was still the weekend. She'd spent all of Saturday watching video after video on the internet showing how to kill a chicken at home. She'd learned that a sharp knife, a firm hand, would minimize the chicken's pain and prevent it from running around the backyard with blood spouting and a partially severed head flopping about.

She stepped out to the backyard with a stainless-steel bowl and her sharpest knife, which she sharpened further against the concrete step that led down from the kitchen. She held the knife in front of her face. She was pleased at the glint of the blade, the way it grazed the skin of her palm with the threat of blood.

As Uzoma approached the chicken, she could feel Nedu gazing at her from his upstairs bedroom window. Sometimes she worried she was failing her children, raising them too soft. There Nedu was, acting like a great tragedy was about to befall him. The other day, he'd untied the chicken's tether and snuck the bird into the house. He'd almost reached the second floor before Uzoma caught him. He stared back at her with wet eyes, mouth gaping open like his lips were made of melting wax. When she asked what Nedu was doing, he said he wanted to give the chicken a shower. It was almost funny. She made Nedu return the chicken to the backyard and watched as he retied the tether. "All roads lead to where?" she'd said. "To your pepper soup pot," Nedu responded, with an incongruous gravity, as if he wouldn't lick clean the bowl of pepper soup she'd place before him when all of this was over and the smell of uziza and scent leaf filled the house. And now here Cherish was, fluttering around Uzoma with her phone's camera recording. She wanted to point out to her daughter that at age fourteen she herself had been attending school *and* working part-time at a big supermarket in Awka. And yet Cherish sat around all day, pressing phone like it was paid work.

Uzoma untied and retied her wrapper around her waist. The chicken was staring her down with its single eye. Her pot of water, to dunk the body in after the deed was done, was simmering on the stove. Her knife was sharp enough to cut breeze. She took a breath. It was time.

Uzoma placed the knife on the ground and returned to the house, ignoring Cherish's "Where are you going?" She went to find her husband in the study. When she opened the door, he snapped his laptop shut.

"Husby, sorry o . . . are you busy?"

He was probably watching porn. She didn't care about his occasional indulgence, but she would never tell him this. She thought it potentially useful to make a man feel like he had more to be guilty about than he really did. And her husband, he was see-through, with his guileless face, his lack of ego—a thing she at once loved and despised about him. It was this lack of ego that had freed him to pursue her without shame, his besotted heart adorning his sleeve for the world to see. It was what made him the children's preferred parent. Not that they'd ever said as much to her; they wouldn't dare. But it was clear from the way they gravitated toward him, offering him jokes and jabs they would never send her way. He was particularly good with Cherish, who seemed to grow further away from her mother as her young body filled out. Wasn't it only a year or so ago that she and Cherish would spend Sunday afternoons watching movies on Africa Magic and taking turns scratching dandruff from each other's scalps? Now, Cherish preferred to sit for hours with her father while they each scrolled through their individual social media pages; every once in a while, one of them would thrust their phone in the other's face and they'd laugh in sync, their heads colliding. And Nedu. How her husband indulged him, rallying her and Cherish to attend that silly naming ceremony for the chicken, breaking the peanuts Nedu had offered as if they were the kola nuts one would serve at a child's naming.

Uzoma told herself there were advantages to having parents with different styles, one with a gentle touch, one to lay down the law. But sometimes she would hear the echoes of laughter in the house and feel her heart sink, knowing from experience that if she tried to join in, the laughter would sputter into silence. She'd learned to comfort herself with her practicality, her sheer usefulness. She was the one the kids came to when they suddenly remembered on a Sunday night that they needed sheets of cardboard paper for school on Monday. She was the one who could tell, before Cherish could, that the pain pulsing in her daughter's abdomen, the fist clenching and unclenching, was heralding her first period. She was the one who'd hunted down Panadol Extra and soda water after midnight while her husband slept.

As Uzoma watched her husband watch her, she decided that he, too, had grown to over-rely on her. Why else would he assume that *she* would be the one to kill the chicken? Why should she have to kill an entire animal when she had an entire man in the house? She could picture him telling her, without shame, sorry, he had never killed a chicken before and he didn't feel like starting today. Just like he'd been without shame that day—what was it, two months ago?—when that lousy policeman had taken their family to the police station and made Ebube lie flat on the ground and beg before they were allowed to leave. She remembered how the officer had stopped their car that afternoon at the checkpoint, how his belly strained against the black police-issue belt, how unbothered he'd seemed by her threats to call her friend, the wife of the police commissioner, to report his demand for "weekend allowance." No such friend existed, but the officer had no way of knowing this. Still, he stood very calm as she plucked her phone from her handbag and waved it at him through the car window that she'd refused to roll down beyond a crack. He regarded her with eyes that looked half-open, as though he couldn't be bothered to give her his full attention. "Madam," he said, his voice unhurried, even playful. "You can return that phone to your bag. You have phone and mouth, I have gun and bullet." And then, to her utmost horror, he'd winked at her! Or she'd imagined him winking at her? She would never be sure. The toothpick in the corner of the officer's mouth bobbed, and a pink slice of tongue slipped out to moisten his bottom lip. She looked away, let the phone fall back into her bag. It was at this point that the officer got into the back of their car—Cherish and Nedu squished themselves in a corner and left a wide space between their bodies and the officer's—and ordered her husband to drive, giving him directions to a police station at Onipanu.

Uzoma and her husband hadn't had sex since then. At first, it was because he was angry at her—he didn't speak to her for the rest of that day! But even after his anger faded, after he started reaching for her again, her body would curl into itself like a disturbed millipede. Each time his hands grazed the insides of her thighs, she would think of those same hands flat on the ground outside the police station, those hands that had come away darkened with dirt after he'd prostrated before the policeman, so low that sand kissed his forehead, and her thighs would clench closed. She'd imagine him thrusting on top of her and cringe at how similar that motion was to him pushing off the ground when the policeman finally gave him permission to stand. He'd even managed to smile with Officer Toothpick after the whole thing, after the policeman had warned him to control his wife or she would get him in trouble one day. "Officer, I don already dey the trouble," her husband had said, his laughter loud like fireworks as the policeman slapped him on the back. You'd think they were old friends.

It was bad enough, this new aversion to her husband's touch, for no reason that made sense. But, to compound her frustrations and further unseat her sense of self, her wayward brain chose to entertain thoughts of that horrible police officer while she lathered herself in the shower, or as she stirred pancake batter, or in those formless moments just before sleep claimed her. She imagined him putting her in handcuffs, making her kneel, prodding that saliva-moistened toothpick with his tongue, grabbing her by the back of the head, telling her to put that foul mouth of hers to good use. By the time she caught herself, there'd be a creeping wetness between her legs. Yet, for her own husband she was dry like dead skin.

Uzoma looked away from her husband, who was now leaning forward in his chair. She imagined he could suddenly see into her depraved depths, see that there was something very wrong with her. She imagined his insides filling with disgust.

. . .

EBUBE FELT A LOT OF THINGS in the moments after his wife appeared before him, but disgust was not one of them. First, Ebube felt surprised—Uzoma usually knocked, but there she was standing inside the study door in her T-shirt and her wrapper snug around her hips. Then there was a twinge of shame. Before his wife showed up, he'd been festering in a cloud of self-pity, troubling Google with queries: *Wife sex drive vanished. How to turn wife on. Why won't wife have sex with me?* His search history wouldn't spark any fires in his wife's loins, that was for sure. And then came annoyance, at Uzoma and the new agility with which she shrank from his touch.

But his annoyance was short-lived. Something in his wife's stance, in her voice as she said, "Husby," was causing him to melt.

He made his voice soft. "I'm not busy. Do you need something?"

She took a step into the room, said not to worry, it was nothing. Then she was gone.

Ebube stared at his closed laptop. He tried to remember the exact time they'd last had sex, but he couldn't pin it down. They definitely hadn't had sex since the day of Tosin's wedding, which they'd ended up missing because his darling wife wouldn't keep her mouth shut and let him grease that officer's waiting palm, like most Lagosians, most Nigerians, did literally every day. Was she still angry at him for humoring the chubby policeman when he'd made that joke about putting a leash on her? See, that was her problem, she'd never understood the little things normal people did to defuse situations, to oil the wheels of ordinary interaction. It was why she had so few friends, why his mother had never quite warmed to her, pleading with him up until a week before their wedding to reconsider. "You are too soft for that woman," his mother had warned.

His mother was wrong. His wife's self-reliance, which his mother read as hardness, didn't bother him; it drew him to her like a spell. And over the years, even as the excitement of their union mellowed and settled into normalcy, the dexterity with which she managed their lives continued to amaze him. But some days he understood his mother's reservations. He could imagine Uzoma getting suddenly bored with him and marching out of his life. She'd demonstrated many times that she didn't need him. She hadn't needed him when she'd started her accounting business. Or when she'd gone into early labor with

Nedu and driven herself to the hospital while he was trapped in Third Mainland Bridge after-work traffic. And now she'd shown it again. Whatever she'd needed, whatever had made her stand before him for those few seconds, she would go take charge of it, as though the sight of him sitting flaccid in his chair had fed new resolve into her bones.

. . .

THAT EVENING, EBUBE, NEDU, AND CHERISH congregated around the dinner table.

"What are we having?" Ebube asked.

"Rice," Nedu said.

"With chicken stew?" Ebube asked hopefully.

"Mum couldn't kill the chicken," Cherish said. "Lol."

"Cherish, you know you're allowed to just laugh," Ebube said, tucking the nugget of information about the still-alive chicken in a corner of his mind.

"Ha ha ha," Cherish said. Ebube shook his head in mock disapproval.

"Dad, Mum couldn't kill Otuanya because he's now part of the family," Nedu said. "His name is Otuanya Isichie."

"I know," Ebube said. "I was at the naming."

"The next time we take a family portrait," Cherish said, "Otuanya can sit on Nedu's head; it's kuku shaped like a nest."

Uzoma walked in from the kitchen holding a serving bowl filled with stew, in time to catch the laughter from Ebube and Cherish. "What's the joke?" she asked merrily.

"Nothing," Cherish said.

Cherish noticed her mother lower her eyes to the floor, the subtle pucker of her mouth. She felt a pinch of remorse. But if Cherish told the joke, her mother would think she was the butt of it, that her family was mocking her for Otuanya's continued state of aliveness. Instead of playing along, she might point out the impracticalities of preparing a chicken to pose for a family photograph, the same way she sucked the fun, like marrow out of bone, from every meme or viral video Cherish dared to share with her. It wasn't Cherish's fault that her mother's sense of humor was fixated on the likes of Aki and Pawpaw and their fellow Nollywood pranksters.

Cherish couldn't believe she used to sit through those silly movies with her mother. The woman became an entirely different person once the opening credits began, with her honking laugh and running commentary. "These boys will soon tackle the old man to the ground . . . Cherish, lekwa, lekwa . . ." Cherish would groan, "Mummy, I'm seeingggg." Still, she'd enjoyed those afternoons, not for the movies themselves but because of her mother's childlike engagement with them, her overreactions to plot twists even when they watched reruns.

If only her mother could be that person all the time. Easy. Maybe then Cherish could tell her about Afolabi, the boy she liked; ask her why, whenever he came close, it suddenly felt like her limbs belonged to someone else. And also, maybe that thing with the police officer would never have happened. She'd held Nedu's hand that afternoon and looked away from the spectacle of her dad lying on the ground begging the officer while her mother stood aside, defiant and arms folded. On the drive home she'd felt the force of her father's anger, so rare, so alien, that it sat on him like a costume that kept slipping off to reveal glimpses of the familiar person hidden inside it. The way he'd slammed on the brakes, the curses he threw at the other drivers who were too slow or too stupid and needed to park their cars at home before they killed someone. Cherish hadn't forgiven her mother for that day. Not that Uzoma would ever ask.

Uzoma placed the bowl of stew on the table with a little more force than Cherish thought was necessary and headed back into the kitchen, calling over her shoulder, "You people can keep laughing, or you can help set the table. Whichever you think is best."

. . .

OF THE MANY POSSIBLE REASONS offered by the internet know-it-alls for his wife's recent coldness in the bedroom, one listicle item from an obscure Christian website worried Ebube's mind like a flickering neon sign: *She's lost respect for you.*

Are you a poor decision-maker? A bad father? Riddled with vices?

Ebube was none of those things. Yes, Uzoma made most of the household decisions, but she liked it that way. It was easier for everyone. And he was a great father; the kids adored him! Even Cherish, who was in her so-called difficult teen years. He did worry about Nedu sometimes: What kind of child got teary-eyed at the pretend naming ceremony for a chicken? And vices . . . well, if you wanted to call them that, sure. But "riddled with" wasn't the way he'd describe his relationship to them.

Cowardly?

His behavior with the police officer was not a show of cowardice. That was him doing what was needed to get his family out of an unnecessary altercation. But he could see how someone—someone like Uzoma, perhaps—might read it as cowardly.

The judgy listicle had called for self-reflection. Perhaps there was something Ebube could do to arouse some respect from Uzoma. A plan began to form in his mind, one that wasn't entirely selfish. First, he'd do some research on chicken slaughter. He'd pick a time when his wife was busy in the kitchen. He would stroll to the backyard and be nonchalant. At the tail end of a yawn and a stretch, he would offer to kill the chicken for her. Casually. Like it was an afterthought.

He practiced in front of the bedroom mirror.

Yawn, stretch. "Ah, Uzoma, Otuanya still hasn't entered your soup pot?" No, too playful. She could interpret this as mockery.

Yawn, stretch. "Uzoma, you know, I can help you kill the chicken." Too direct. She might take it as a challenge.

Yawn, stretch. "Uzoma, ngwa, bring a knife and let me kill this chicken." No, too authoritative. He'd never pull that off.

How about no yawn, no stretch: "Uzoma, I think you're having a hard time killing the chicken. I say this because you've been bent on making chicken pepper soup for weeks. Would you like me to handle it? You don't have to do everything all the time. You'd still be a wonder to me."

He discarded the idea. Uzoma would hate that.

He would just go into the kitchen and begin sharpening a knife, ask his wife to put a large pot of water on the fire. She would get it. Her eyes would tear up with gratitude. And so, after fortifying himself with chicken-killing knowledge, he went into the kitchen, began sharpening a knife, asked his wife to put a large pot of water on the fire. Her eyes did not tear up.

"Have you killed a chicken before?" she asked.

"Have you?"

She regarded him in silence for a moment. "Thank you," she said.

She was welcome. She didn't need to know how many videos he'd watched in preparation, or that his goals went beyond helping to manifest Otuanya's destiny.

"But not now," his wife said. "It's too hot outside."

He agreed. "We'll do it in the evening."

"Do what?" Nedu asked as he walked into the kitchen.

Ebube hesitated. If Nedu were a different kind of boy, this might be a chance to teach him something; something about doing difficult things, maybe? It wasn't entirely clear to Ebube how to frame the death of a chicken as a teachable moment. "I'm going to kill the chicken."

Nedu's face looked stricken. "You're still killing Otuanya?"

Ebube tried to be gentle. "Nedu, your mother has been talking about making chicken pepper soup for weeks; which chicken did you think was going to feature in the soup?"

"But . . . he's one of us now," Nedu said. "All of you came to his naming!"

Cherish appeared in the kitchen doorway. "Nedu," she said. "It's not a 'he,' it's an 'it,' and *it* is a chicken."

As Nedu turned and ran toward the stairs, Uzoma saw an opportunity for a joke. She called after her son, "Nedu, the chicken will fully become one with our family when he dwells inside our tummies!" She laughed too loud, hoping her husband and daughter would join in, but her laughter died alone.

. . .

AS THE SUN STARTED TO SET, Uzoma prepared the tools for Otuanya's slaughter. She hoped Nedu would stay in his room; she didn't want any drama. She briefly worried that killing the chicken might traumatize the boy, but she dismissed that thought. It was only a chicken. By the time the pepper soup was ready, Nedu would have forgotten the bird's name.

The whole family gathered in the kitchen, except for Nedu. A large pot of water bubbled on the stove. Ebube girded himself. Cherish, with her phone out, camera recording, asked, "Dad, are you ready to slay?"

"Ready," Ebube said.

Uzoma snorted with mild derision, but the laughter in her eyes warmed Ebube's heart. Uzoma grabbed the knife and they all stepped out into the backyard. But under the wrapper-canopy where the chicken should have been, there was nothing. The length of rope that had tethered the bird to the clothesline had been snipped in half. Uzoma could think of only one culprit.

"Neduuuu!"

"Shh, shh, shh," Ebube said. "Look."

He pointed, and his wife and daughter followed his finger toward the gate, where Otuanya stood, the other half of the tether trailing on the ground. The chicken was at the threshold of the pedestrian gate, which stood wide open. Otuanya was perched on one leg, the other poised to land on the ground, on the other side of the gate. The chicken turned and skewered the family with that single eye before disappearing across the threshold.

The trio chased the chicken down the street. The few people they passed gave them a wide berth, ignoring Uzoma's cries to "Catch that chicken!"

Near the end of the street, the bird launched itself over a low wall and into a compound with a white house and hibiscus hedges. Without hesitation, Uzoma banged on the gate, and when a bewildered gateman opened, she barged in. "I must cook that pepper soup today!"

They found Otuanya cowering by a banana tree behind the house, legs entangled in the tether. The family left with their prize secured in Ebube's grip.

• • •

THAT EVENING, THE SMELL OF Otuanya's destiny filled the house and woke Nedu from his angry nap. But when his mother called him to come down for dinner, he stayed in his bed. Nedu imagined his family, betrayers and murderers all of them, sitting down to eat his friend, not caring that there was literal blood on their hands, blood in their stomachs, and blood on their fangs. They were animals.

His mother sent Cherish up to get him.

"I'm not eating," Nedu said.

When Cherish reported Nedu's response, Uzoma felt a twinge of worry. Nedu never refused food. He ate with a fearsome appetite, meals disappearing into his skinny body like stolen evidence. She decided to be annoyed.

"Imagine Nedu releasing the chicken so we wouldn't eat it," she said. "What he deserves is a spanking, not my delicious pepper soup."

. . .

THERE HAD BEEN A SUBTLE HEAT in his wife's gaze all evening, but Ebube stifled his hope. He didn't want to reach for Uzoma and be rebuffed again. When it was time for bed, he got under the covers and turned his back to her, even though she was wearing that chemise he liked, the one with the red pouted lips all over it, the one whose bodice cupped her small breasts like a prayer.

He felt the sigh of the mattress as she joined him on the bed. And then her hand was on his shirtless shoulder, traveling slowly down his back. Ebube's eyes flew open.

"Bubu," she said, the mist of her breath tickling his ear. She hadn't called him that in ages. "The way you handled that chicken today ehn . . . I was very impressed."

Ebube turned toward her. "Really?"

She took his hand and guided it between her legs. "The way you took control . . ."

In one fluid motion—one that Ebube hadn't known he was still capable of—he launched himself on top of his wife and pinned her hands above her head. Uzoma yelped, the sound of her laughter bouncing off the walls.

Ebube clamped a hand over his wife's mouth. "Shhh . . . the children."

She shrugged an I-don't-care and licked the inside of his palm. Maybe she was being a little reckless, but they'd lived in that house long enough to know that the walls weren't thin. He unclamped her mouth, placed a quick kiss on her lips, and rolled off her.

She held on to his arm. "Where are you going?"

"To lock the door."

Her grip tightened. "Don't."

He laughed. "One of the kids might come in."

"They won't."

Cherish would be on her phone, and Nedu was either still sulking or had devoured the food she'd left outside his door and was now in a post-meal stupor. Either way, Uzoma was sure her children wouldn't show up at their bedroom door. Like ninety-two percent sure. There was something about that eight percent uncertainty, though, the danger it represented, that was doing things to her insides. She wanted Ebube to revel with her in the eight percent, to hold her hands above her head again and make her do every single thing he'd ever been afraid to want.

"Why risk it, though?" He pried his arm free and rolled off the bed. The lock clicked into place. "Much better. Now, where were we?"

Ebube's eyes fell on the bed, on the wall of Uzoma's back now turned against him. He lowered his body carefully beside hers. He asked if everything was okay. She said yes. If he believed her, he'd have the courage to reach for her again, to try to tease out the Uzoma who, just moments ago, was aligning her body with his, taking his hand and leading him places. A space was opening up between them, vast and treacherous. He was too tired to navigate. A soft sadness enveloped him.

"What did I do?"

Uzoma sighed. She had no words to account for her new appetites. Her blooming perversions. These thoughts of moist toothpicks and black uniforms.

"Nothing," she said. "You did nothing."

. . .

UZOMA HAD BEEN RIGHT. The children were occupied. In Cherish's room, footage of the chicken chase was being intently edited, with added music and sound effects. She kept the video's caption simple: "Epic chicken chase." Cherish watched the likes and comments pop up on her phone, each one giving a little thrill. She whispered a thank you to God or the universe for giving her the idea to cut Otuanya's tether.

Cherish saw a like from Afolabi, and then a comment: [Laughing-crying emoji] omg @CisforCherish your family is comedy goals fr!!!!

Did Afolabi mean *comedy goals* or *comedy gold*? Did it matter? All Cherish knew was that her video had made Afolabi laugh. With four exclamation points! Warmth invaded her face, her chest, spreading like fire, claiming territory. On the last day of the school term, standing in line behind him at assembly, she'd pressed her finger to the mole on the back of his neck, something she'd been wanting to do ever since she'd discovered it peeking over the horizon of his uniform collar like a dark, shy sun. He'd turned to her with a quizzical frown, and she'd mouthed *sorry* and looked away, her stomach quivering with shame. She was sure he'd avoid all interaction with her from that day till forever, but here he was liking her video. Cherish cradled her phone to her heart. She gazed at the ceiling. When they kissed for the first time, she would poke her tongue between the gap in his front teeth.

Meanwhile, Nedu had just woken from a second nap, a hungry nap, and he remembered that Otuanya was gone. Well, not gone *gone*, not exactly. He was still around, in his mother's soup pot, his final resting place. Nedu's stomach growled, reminding him that some things he couldn't escape. Like hunger. He had taken a stand without thinking, and now, as the pangs pulled at his insides, he hoped none of his family was still downstairs. He didn't want to encounter anyone when he went scrounging for food in the kitchen.

He opened his bedroom door. A tray with a plate of pounded yam and a bowl of pepper soup had been left there, on the floor beside the door, for him. The pepper soup had a light film over it. The food would be cold by now, the white ball of pounded yam slightly hard on the surface. Nedu wondered if it might be okay to still eat the food his mother had made, without actually eating any of Otuanya. He could eat *around* Otuanya.

Nedu lifted the tray, careful not to make a sound, and retreated into his room, closing the door quietly behind him. He placed the tray on the floor at the foot of his bed and sat before it. From the pepper soup bowl, a large piece of Otuanya confronted him, and Nedu was distressed to realize that he didn't remember which side of the chicken's head had the missing eye. He dipped a finger into the pepper soup. Yes, he would eat around Otuanya. He popped the soup-covered finger into his mouth and sucked on it. His eyes and mouth flooded with liquid as the flavors registered on his tongue, that hint of ginger his mother always added to her pepper soup.

When Nedu tells the story to his family, days later, he will say he left his body, and that by the time he came back, the pounded yam had disappeared, the pepper soup bowl was licked dry, and the chewed-up bones of Otuanya's leg were littering the tray. He will be sincere, and when his mother smiles and calls him her food warrior, when she says she knew he would forget about his chicken friend and make her proud, he will decide that the rest of the story—the part where he'd hidden in the bathroom and stuck a finger down his throat to bring Otuanya back up and into the toilet bowl—will stay with him. That part he will keep for himself.

MILK AND OIL

IT WASN'T THAT MILK, IN ITSELF, WAS STRANGE TO Chekwube. She used evaporated milk to brighten tea, to thin akamu and custard for breakfast. She stole fistfuls of powdered milk from the kitchen cupboard and hid behind her bedroom door to lick her hands clean. But she had never seen a real-life person drink milk from a tall glass. Chekwube had thought that only white children on TV drank milk this way, like it was water. And so she stared as Soty stood in her bedroom guzzling down the glass of milk Aunty Ngozi had just handed to her. Whitish chunks clung to the inside of the glass, small undissolved blobs of powdered milk that Chekwube longed to mash with her tongue. The room was silent, except for the glugs of Soty's swallows and the soft clinking of her teeth against the glass.

Chekwube had first met Soty several weeks ago, when Mrs. Ejiofor introduced Soty, newly enrolled at Motunde Memorial Primary School, to the Primary Five B class and led her to the empty seat beside Chekwube. Even though they were now best friends—a tacit understanding of this fact had grown between them after the first few times Soty reached across to Chekwube's desk and left offerings in the form of snacks—Soty remained strange to Chekwube. Chekwube had noticed, for instance, that she made a point of avoiding the sun, adhering to shadows like she was allergic to light. On their walks from school, Soty never strayed from the shade of Aunty Ngozi's large umbrella, which was not big enough to also accommodate Chekwube's body. And how about the loose-knit cardigan that Soty always brought with her to school, no matter how warm the day? When she wasn't wearing the purple cardigan, she had it tied around her waist, the sleeves knotted into an oversized navel.

Chekwube remembered the first time she'd watched Soty eat a green apple. Soty had started by using her teeth to gently scrape off the film of skin until the whole apple lay bare and white. Then she'd taken small, even bites of apple flesh and sucked the juice out of it, chewing and swallowing only when it had become husk in her mouth. She hadn't seemed to mind that the apple quickly turned an unsightly brown with exposure, or that Chekwube had been doing her best to keep from slapping the apple out of her hand. Still, despite this strange behavior, Chekwube had found herself drawn to the oddling. Every day, when the bell rang for lunch break, they would pool their snacks on Soty's desk and divide them equally: Okin biscuits, baba dudus, and groundnuts from Chekwube, and Smarties, Nasco wafers, and Ribena from Soty. The Ribena proved tricky to share equally; they each took turns sucking from the straw while the other counted to five.

Earlier that afternoon, while Mrs. Ejiofor drew a misshapen map of Nigeria on the blackboard, Soty had leaned close to Chekwube's ear and invited Chekwube to her home after school. When Aunty Ngozi showed up to walk Soty home, Soty shared the news of Chekwube's impending visit and Aunty Ngozi's mouth tightened into a raisin. Before that day, Chekwube had barely paid any attention to Aunty Ngozi, who never said or did much for Chekwube to pay attention to. Aunty Ngozi was short and solemn, with full, slightly pockmarked cheeks and an expressive mouth that seemed to be the sole outlet for her emotions. The threaded lengths of her hair looked like vines growing out of her skull, with multiple vines bound together into thicker trunks that either curved down toward her back or sat atop her head like a crown, depending on the style she was wearing. The entire walk home that afternoon, Aunty Ngozi was silent, her lips stiff and unyielding as a ruler. Chekwube decided she wasn't going to like her.

Soty lived in a quiet part of Isolo, on a street with only one way in and out, and a gate that closed to vehicles of nonresidents after 8:00 PM. At the entrance to the street, there was a small gatehouse with a sour-faced gateman. Unlike at Chekwube's apartment—which was located in a building at the top of a T junction near Mushin Road, across from a loading point for Okota- and Mushin-bound danfos—there were no buses in sight. Every morning, Chekwube woke up to a chorus of bus conductors and agberos calling on passengers with voices raspy from weed and struggle. But Soty probably woke up to the sound of birds. The outside of Soty's building was painted dark green, and the walls felt bumpy to the touch, like the paint had been mixed with sand. The compound was surrounded by a dusty breeze-block wall topped with shards of broken glass to discourage burglars. There were four apartments in the building; Soty's was one of two on the ground floor.

Inside, the apartment smelled of boiling tomatoes and old AC air. Even though there was no electricity that afternoon, it was cool inside the living room, and heavy, dark curtains blocked out most of the heat and light of the sun. As Chekwube's eyes adjusted to the dimness, she could make out a large TV on a display shelf and framed pictures dotting the walls. Soty shrugged off her backpack and flung it onto an overstuffed armchair, dark red to match the carpet. Aunty Ngozi disappeared under an archway past the dining area.

"Let's go to my room," Soty said, taking Chekwube's hand and leading her down a corridor. They emerged into a room with walls and gauzy curtains in shades of purple. The bed was neatly made, with too many pillows and a large purple blanket that looked painfully soft. There was a white dresser with drawer handles shaped like flowers, and on top of it a jewelry box bursting with colorful bead necklaces and earrings. Soty showed Chekwube her collection of seashells. "We went to Bar Beach this year for my birthday. Look, nine shells for my nine years." The shells were in a large glass jar half filled with white sand and purple glitter. The biggest shell was almost the size of Chekwube's hand. Soty lifted the jar and shook it gently. The shells appeared to be playing hide-and-seek with each other, amid all that sand and glitter and, though she didn't understand why, when Soty handed her the jar to shake, Chekwube imagined herself hurling it against the wall, watching sand and purple glitter shimmer down to the floor. If Aunty Ngozi hadn't walked in with the glass of milk at that moment, Chekwube wondered, would she have smashed the jar?

Soty finished her milk and handed the empty glass back to Aunty Ngozi. When Aunty Ngozi left the room, Chekwube asked Soty, "Why are you drinking milk?"

"For my bones," Soty said, like she was the only one with bones.

When Aunty Ngozi returned moments later, it was bath time. Aunty Ngozi pulled Soty's uniform over her head. It was no news to Chekwube that Soty was skinny, but her body looked even smaller naked than it did with clothes on. She was made of hard edges: a pointy chin, sharp knees and elbows, ribs that jutted like splayed fingers. Aunty Ngozi kneeled before Soty and unbuckled her school shoes, pulled off her socks. Chekwube undressed herself, feeling a swell of pride in her chest because she didn't need any help. They walked down the corridor to a bathroom with green tiles and a green tub. In the center of the tub was a large basin of water with a pouring bowl floating in the middle. Soty and Chekwube got into the tub on opposite sides of the bowl, and Chekwube dipped her hand into the warm water and swirled it around to make a storm. Aunty Ngozi swatted at her hand.

Chekwube soaped herself while Aunty Ngozi scrubbed Soty's torso with a soft sponge that left a trail of strawberry-scented foam wherever it touched. Chekwube eyed the sponge with a mix of disdain and suspicion. It would not remove dirt; it would just move the dirt around. Her trusty kankan sponge at home, made of straw fiber, was the only thing that could rub skin raw and clean.

When Soty's body was covered with fluffy foam, she swiped a dollop from her buttocks and flicked it at Chekwube. "My bum-bum foam is on your face!"

Chekwube pretended to be horrified. She threw a handful of water in Soty's face and some of it got into her nose. Soty sputtered and started to cough. Chekwube was getting ready to deploy a second missile when Aunty Ngozi snapped, "Stop that!"

"Soty started it!"

Soty coughed louder, so loud Chekwube suspected she was faking it. But Aunty Ngozi patted her back and soothed her until she grew quiet.

Back in Soty's bedroom, Aunty Ngozi set a tub of body lotion before Chekwube. Then she hurried out of the room and returned with a large bottle of Goya olive oil. She poured some of the golden liquid into a cupped palm, rubbed her hands together and began massaging the oil onto Soty's skin. The oil had the smell of old grass, and Chekwube watched, mesmerized, as Aunty Ngozi covered Soty in it, lingering on knees, elbows, and ankles, carefully rubbing behind ears and between fingers and toes. When all of Soty was shiny with oil, Aunty Ngozi filled the cap of the bottle.

"Aaahh," Aunty Ngozi said.

Soty turned her head away, moving in the opposite direction of Aunty Ngozi's hand and the bottle cap.

"Soty," Aunty Ngozi said, half pleading, half warning. Soty closed her eyes and said *aaahh*, and Aunty Ngozi fed her the oil, muttering something about Jesus's blood. Aunty Ngozi watched Soty carefully, making sure she'd swallowed it all, before leaving with the bottle.

"What was all that?" Chekwube asked.

"Healing olive oil from Aunty Ngozi's church," Soty said. She wiped her mouth. "My mummy doesn't like her giving it to me."

"Why is she giving you healing oil?"

"She says the oil will transform my sickler blood into the blood of Jesus." Chekwube's confusion must have shown on her face because Soty continued. "I have sickle cell."

"What's sickle cell?"

Soty hesitated. "It's like . . ." She shook her head. "Don't worry, it's nothing."

Chekwube had more questions, but she swallowed them when Aunty Ngozi reappeared. While Aunty Ngozi busied herself picking out clothes for the girls from Soty's drawer, Chekwube swiped a fingertip on Soty's naked stomach and it came away slick with oil. When Soty wasn't looking, Chekwube popped the finger in her mouth and sucked it dry.

· · ·

THE NEXT TIME SOTY BROUGHT a green apple to school for lunch, it was precut into two neat halves. Soty taught Chekwube how to eat the apple her way. Chekwube had learned by this time that Soty was a picky eater when it came to meals, proficient at finding excuses not to finish the food on her plate, to Aunty Ngozi's frustration—the onions in her fried eggs were cut too big, the beans weren't soft enough, the plantains were too salty. The eating of snacks was where Soty excelled. She had a method for each kind. With biscuits, she nibbled off the edges first, working her way, in spiral fashion, toward the center; with wafers, she separated the layers and licked off the sweet cream in between. She sucked the color off the hard, crunchy shells of her Smarties and mashed the chocolate into a paste that she spread onto cabin biscuits. Chekwube learned the subtle pleasures of eating this way, of savoring one component before the next, saving the best part for last. Some days, the consumption of their snacks took up the entire forty minutes of their lunch break.

On the days when Soty let Chekwube coax her outside, they would find a spot under the neem trees that lined the school fence, and Chekwube would teach Soty to play suwe and ten-ten. When they teamed up and played against other girls, they lost more often than they won. After every loss, each girl would blame the other, resulting in a fight that lasted only till the bell rang at the end of break. Some days, they spent break time huddled at Soty's desk, eating quietly, with Soty's purple sweater draped over their heads. Soty would take out her fancy purple notebook and divide fresh pages into panels like comic strips. Before they'd become friends, Chekwube had observed Soty with the sweater over her head and the book before her, scrawling and muttering to herself. She'd always assumed Soty was studying and resented her furtiveness, her arrogance at thinking that the whole world was interested in her business. But now, Chekwube knew that Soty filled the pages with drawings, that she'd started drawing once when she was in the hospital for weeks, bored. The drawings were little more than stick figures, but Soty was good at piecing them together to create stories, all of which featured an intergalactic hero called Super S.

With the cardigan covering their heads, the world became tinged purple. There was confidence in Soty's pen strokes and in the stories that accompanied them, and during these drawing sessions Chekwube would find herself entranced, following the lines as ink poured and pooled from the tip of Soty's Eleganza pen to stain the page with mystery and adventure. She inhaled the scent of the ink mixed with the milky smell of Soty's breath while Soty narrated the stories in hot whispers: Super S saves a trio of princesses from a witch who held them zombified in her cave, where she cut off their hair and made it into wigs and drank their blood as tea. Super S uncovers a nefarious plot by a recurring villain, Oga Doom, to enslave the entire galaxy. Super S fights killer monsters with heads like dark crescent moons.

. . .

ONE SATURDAY, CHEKWUBE'S MOTHER VISITED Soty's mother's store in a shopping complex across from Saint Mary's Church. With Chekwube and Soty glued together, she had grown curious about their friendship, and had begun to pepper Chekwube with questions: "What do her parents do? Why haven't I met her mother?"

As they stood in the store, Chekwube watched her mother dutifully admire the lengths of fabric, and the necklaces and bracelets heavy with precious and semiprecious stones that Mrs. Onwuchekwa put in her hands while she recited provenance—lace from Italy, gold from Dubai. "Is there anything specific you're looking for?" she asked. Chekwube's mother didn't answer, returned every item with a tight smile and vague promises of "another day."

Chekwube's mother was not the kind of woman who appreciated the things that women did to make themselves look and feel pretty. She wore a rotation of the same five gray suits to her job at a microfinance bank—the company colors were gray and orange—and abstained from events that required her to buy aso-ebi or wear matching hairstyles: "If my presence is not enough, I can stay in my house." Mrs. Onwuchekwa, in contrast, loved colorful boubous and filmy robes that rippled and shimmered with her every movement. With her merry eyes and trilling laugh, she must have grated on Chekwube's mother's more somber sensibilities. It was a short visit. By the time she and her mother had returned home from the store, having exchanged very few words on their way back, Chekwube could tell that there would be no great friendship between the two women.

. . .

"WHEN CAN I COME to your house?" The question came from Soty during one of their afternoon drawing sessions, right after Super S won yet another victory against Oga Doom. Chekwube had known this question was coming, was inevitable. Still, she'd been dreading the day Soty would ask. So far, the girls had only ever spent time at Soty's. When they had sleepovers, both girls nestled in Soty's bed, under her blanket, nibbling on snacks they'd stolen from the kitchen cupboards. Only Aunty Ngozi had seen where Chekwube lived, and only from the outside, on days when she walked Chekwube home from Soty's late in the evening.

"Whenever you like," Chekwube said in a voice she hoped was casual enough to hide the pounding of her heart.

When Soty came to play at Chekwube's house, they played quietly. It was a Saturday and Chekwube's mother was at home with a migraine. There was no electricity to watch TV, so they played X and O and tried to tune Chekwube's fussy handheld radio to find music. They wandered downstairs behind the building to play suwe. They went back inside to snack on cabin biscuits and orange-flavored Tasty Time and then showed each other their tongues, bright orange from the juice concentrate. The whole time, Chekwube's eyes followed wherever Soty's went. Was it just her, or did Soty's gaze linger on that spot near the living room archway where a hole was forming in the carpet? Did she frown at the torn mosquito net on Chekwube's bedroom window, how it flapped in the breeze? When Soty sprang up from Chekwube's bed and suggested taking the radio outside to try again to make it work, was it because the errant spring in Chekwube's bed had poked her?

Shortly before it was time for her to go home, Soty asked to use the toilet and Chekwube's stomach sank. The first time she'd used the toilet at Soty's house she'd flushed three times, just to relive the joyful cycle of the flushing: the water rushing into the toilet bowl, making everything clean; the merry tinkle of the tank refilling itself; the silence that followed, heavy with the promise of all that water just waiting to be deployed again. Chekwube's building hadn't had running water in years; she'd taken out the float ball from the toilet tank long ago and used it as a toy. Chekwube's mother saved old laundry water to flush with. The water sat in a slimy bucket in the corner of the bathroom and smelled if left too long. They bought clean water from the water seller who came every few days peddling his precious cargo in fifty-liter jerry cans, water too costly for chasing down unwanted things.

Chekwube showed Soty how to flush and then left her alone, certain that their friendship would be over when Soty came out, just like with Olamide from two streets away, who'd stopped looking Chekwube in the eye after she'd used her toilet.

There was the sound of a grunt, and water sloshing into the toilet bowl. Then Soty emerged proud from the toilet. She nodded at Chekwube like she had completed a great task and all was well with the world. Chekwube felt light-headed with shame and relief.

. . .

WITH MRS. ONWUCHEKWA AT HER SHOP one afternoon, and Aunty Ngozi napping, Chekwube and Soty ventured into Mrs. Onwuchekwa's bedroom. The inside of the room was dim and smelled of perfume and Tony Montana powder. It was slightly untidy, with clothes spilling from the lip of a laundry basket and wrappers and laces piled on the bed like someone had left in a hurry. It was the biggest bedroom in the house, with its own bathroom on the side, a washbasin, and countertops that held the creams and potions that kept Mrs. Onwuchekwa's face free of lines. There was a dresser made of dark wood, with a mirror and copious amounts of makeup that smelled chemical and sweet. The dresser drawers would not close properly; they were overstuffed with swaths of fabric peeking out, laces and George wrappers in different colors. A Dansk Danish Cookies tin lay half open on the dresser, filled with loose objects: buttons, sequins and rhinestones, broken clip-on earrings, a lapel pin, a string of fake pearls with peeling skin, needles and rolls of thread, a box of matches.

Soty steered Chekwube to her mother's wardrobe, where there was a stack of books on the top tier. "I want to show you something."

Soty stood on the tips of her toes and counted down the spines of the books. "Remember where I removed this book from," she said, straining. "I must return it to the same place." She plucked a book with a pixelated white woman on the cover. *Everywoman*. The woman had short dark hair and a faraway look in her eyes. She was sitting hugging herself.

They sat inside the door of the wardrobe with their foreheads almost touching. The way Soty flipped to certain pages of *Everywoman*, it was clear she'd done this before. Chekwube was shocked by the diagrams. There was a series of drawings of a fetus with its body curved, shrimplike, in the early stages, then growing till it became a recognizable human baby. On the next page, the baby's head parting vagina lips. The girls squirmed and giggled at the drawings, so far removed from any reality they could imagine for themselves. They picked body parts and made them into insults: *Your head looks like a uterus. Your face like a vagina. Your neck like a fallopian tube.*

The door opened. Soty was quick, tossing the book into the back of the wardrobe with Mrs. Onwuchekwa's shoes.

Aunty Ngozi squinted at them. "What are you girls doing here?"

"Nothing," Soty said.

"Hide-and-seek," Chekwube said at the same time.

"This room is not your playground," Aunty Ngozi said.

"But if we go outside, you'll start shouting up and down, 'Chekwube, Soty,'" Chekwube said. It was the one thing she didn't like about spending time at Soty's house, Aunty Ngozi sequestering them indoors. The few times she'd managed to sneak Soty out of the house, Aunty Ngozi had been quick to sniff them out, whether they went behind the building or huddled beside the tarp-covered vehicle at the far end of the compound that looked like it hadn't moved in years. At least at school they could play outside sometimes, and so far she hadn't seen Soty melt in the sun.

"You know your mum doesn't like you playing outside," Aunty Ngozi said. "You can go and play in your room."

Chekwube felt a spark of inspiration. She leaned in close to Soty and whispered into her ear.

"Mummy also doesn't like you giving me your stinking oil," Soty said to Aunty Ngozi.

Chekwube watched Aunty Ngozi's face for that moment when her lips would fold in on themselves. Aunty Ngozi's eyes fell on Chekwube, but she didn't flinch.

"Okay." Aunty Ngozi sounded constipated. "You can go outside, just for twenty minutes." She listed off a set of rules that included not leaving the compound and "no rough play."

As they left the bedroom, Soty whispered, "Aunty Ngozi, your head looks like a fallopian tube."

"What did you say?" Aunty Ngozi asked.

"Nothing," Soty said, fleeing the room with a chuckling Chekwube at her side.

Outside, Chekwube headed straight for the tree across the street from Soty's house. The fruit had been hanging fat and yellow for weeks, taunting Chekwube. Soty said she'd never had one, and Chekwube shook her head in exaggerated disappointment. "Ordinary ebelebo fruit, you haven't eaten."

While Chekwube looked for sticks suitable for aiming at the ripe fruit, Soty snuck inside to put *Everywoman* back in its place among her mother's books. Soty returned and Chekwube demonstrated how to throw the sticks. When they each had three or four fruits, they arranged them on the ledge of the roadside gutter. Chekwube wiped the fruit on her dress and called Soty an ajebutter when she suggested they go inside to wash them with water and salt. They chewed on the fibrous flesh of the fruit and made it into pink mush that they stuck out on their tongues and let dribble from the corners of their mouths as they fake-convulsed and fake-died like the actors in Nollywood movies. Chekwube showed Soty how to crack the hard shell of the seed to reveal the crunchy kernel inside.

"Do you like it?" Chekwube asked.

Soty nodded vigorously. But when Chekwube got home that evening she found that Soty had snuck the rest of her uneaten fruit into Chekwube's backpack.

The next day, Aunty Ngozi arrived to pick Soty up from school looking even more sullen than usual. On the walk home, Aunty Ngozi said, "Chekwube, Soty said you made her eat fruit from that tree on our street."

Soty and Chekwube spoke at the same time.

"She didn't make me—"

"I didn't make her do anything."

"Why are you so stubborn, Chekwube?" Aunty Ngozi said. "Didn't I tell you not to leave the compound yesterday? You carried Soty and went across the road to—"

"I didn't *carry* her!"

"Shut up when I'm talking! Just because I allowed you girls to go outside, you went and gave her that dirty fruit from the tree. Did you even wash it first?"

Soty looked shrunken with shame beside Aunty Ngozi, under the shade of that umbrella. But Chekwube wanted to kick Aunty Ngozi's legs out from under her, feel the ground shake as she fell.

"See ehn," Aunty Ngozi continued, "if I catch you taking Soty to play nonsense play again, you'll hear from me. No more playing outside for her. You can play by yourself if you don't like it."

"Aunty Ngozi, we're sorry," Soty mumbled.

"Sorry for yourselves," Aunty Ngozi said.

When they were alone in Soty's room, Soty apologized to Chekwube for telling Aunty Ngozi about the fruit. She'd had a bad stomachache, she said, after Chekwube went home, and she'd had to confess to Aunty Ngozi, to give account of everything she'd eaten. Chekwube had no problem with Soty; it was Aunty Ngozi who'd yelled at her, accused her of dragging Soty around as if Soty was a doll baby who couldn't speak for herself. And what was this stomachache business, just because of one ebelebo fruit? Chekwube herself had eaten four! With all that milk Soty drank, you'd think the girl would have tougher organs.

As Soty continued speaking, Chekwube set her mind to planning vengeance on Aunty Ngozi. She told herself to be patient, that it would likely take some time for the right opportunity to present itself. But the very next afternoon, she got her chance. When the girls got back from school, Mrs. Onwuchekwa was already home, which was unusual. After the girls had bathed and Aunty Ngozi had snuck away to get the oil for Soty, Chekwube decided what she would do. But she told herself she would give Aunty Ngozi one more chance at redemption.

When Aunty Ngozi returned with the oil, Chekwube presented herself to her.

"Aunty Ngozi, please do me too," she said, in what she considered to be her sweetest voice.

Aunty Ngozi didn't even spare her a glance. "It's not for you."

Chekwube told herself that it was only anger at Aunty Ngozi that made her body suddenly feel hot all over. It wasn't jealousy, this clenching feeling that settled in the pit of her stomach, even though Aunty Ngozi was confirming that Soty was indeed special, set aside for this oil treatment that Chekwube could not have. And it was Aunty Ngozi she would be punishing, not Soty. Soty didn't even like drinking that oil. If anything, she would be helping Soty, freeing her from Aunty Ngozi's tyranny. It was this thought that propelled Chekwube, still wrapped in a bath towel, into the living room, where Mrs. Onwuchekwa sat counting naira bills and writing in a notebook.

"Aunty Ngozi is forcing Chekwube to drink her healing oil."

Mrs. Onwuchekwa let out a sigh of frustration. She went into Soty's room. Chekwube stood outside the door and listened to Mrs. Onwuchekwa scold Aunty Ngozi: "I've told you to stop giving my child this nonsense oil!"

Chekwube wished she could see Aunty Ngozi's face, ask her how it felt to be on the receiving end. When Mrs. Onwuchekwa left Soty's room, she was holding the large bottle with its golden liquid. She declared she would begin locking her bedroom, with the oil inside it, when she left the house.

Later that evening, Aunty Ngozi ambushed Chekwube in the kitchen. She stood between Chekwube and the doorway, hemming her in. "You this small witch." She spoke softly. Her lips trembled but her voice was firm. "You told Soty's mum about the oil."

Chekwube stared at the space between Aunty Ngozi's eyebrows and said nothing. She hoped Aunty Ngozi would hit her, so she could scream the roof down and cry so hard that maybe Mrs. Onwuchekwa would send Aunty Ngozi away, back to wherever she'd come from.

"Do you know Soty has sickle cell?" Aunty Ngozi said. "You want her to get sick? You think you're very smart, but if anything happens to her, her blood will be on your head."

"Leave me alone," Chekwube yelled, pushing past Aunty Ngozi into the safety of the living room.

. . .

IT WAS A SATURDAY AFTERNOON and Aunty Ngozi was kneading dough for a pizza. Chekwube was mesmerized at how the dough succumbed to the squeezes and pressure of Aunty Ngozi's hands, how it gave in. She wanted to ask if she could stick her fingers in the dough, but since the healing oil incident a few weeks ago, Aunty Ngozi had grown even colder toward her, ignoring her except when communication was unavoidable. Chekwube did not mind this; she reminded herself she didn't like Aunty Ngozi. But now, with her fingers itching to massage the dough, she wondered if she could sweet-talk her. Or perhaps she could poke the dough when Aunty Ngozi wasn't looking.

Soty did not share Chekwube's fascination with the pizza dough. She wanted them to go play in her room.

"I've never eaten pizza before," Chekwube explained.

Soty nudged Aunty Ngozi. "Aunty Ngozi, did you hear? She said *pee-zah*."

Chekwube was confused. "Yes, pizza."

Soty laughed, and Aunty Ngozi joined in. "Bush girl," Soty said. "It's not *pee-zah*, it's *peet-sah*."

Soty and Aunty Ngozi didn't laugh for long, but Chekwube felt like each second of it lasted ten years. The way their bodies leaned into each other as they laughed, at her, Chekwube was convinced they'd done it many times before. They'd laughed at her broken toilet at home and the old laundry water in the slimy bucket. They'd shuddered at the thought of her bedroom swarming with mosquitoes her torn nets failed to keep out, wrinkled their noses at the smell of kerosene smoke that she knew clung to her clothes no matter how long she aired them out.

"*Bush girl. It's not pee-zah, it's peet-sah.*"

Soty went quiet. Her eyes narrowed in a moment of incomprehension. Those were her words coming from Chekwube's mouth, the words formed with Soty's same lisp, the same derision, the same whiny quality. In the time it had taken for their laughter to fade, Chekwube had plotted a revenge that was exquisite in its simplicity.

"What are you doing?" Soty asked.

Chekwube kept her face blank. "*What are you doing?*"

Aunty Ngozi kept kneading her dough, letting out the occasional grunt when she pressed down on it. Soty stood still. Chekwube could feel her testing the air between them.

"Chekwube."

"*Chekwube.*"

"Aunty Ngozi, do you see what Chekwube is doing?"

"*Aunty Ngozi, do you see what Chekwube is doing?*"

Aunty Ngozi attempted a half-hearted intervention. "Chekwube, stop copying her."

As moments passed in silence, Chekwube watched the tension slowly leave her friend's shoulders, watched as the minutes did the work that time did so well. Aunty Ngozi set aside the dough and stirred a pot of tomato sauce bubbling on the gas. Soty stretched out a hand.

"Aunty Ngozi, can I taste?"

"*Aunty Ngozi, can I taste?*"

"Chekwube!"

"*Chekwube!*"

"Aunty Ngozi, can you hear her? She's still doing it!"

"*Aunty Ngozi, can you hear her? She's still doing it!*"

Chekwube watched Soty's face and reveled in her frown, in her frustration.

"Chekwube, stop it, I'm telling you!"

"*Chekwube, stop it, I'm telling you!*"

"Aunty Ngozi, warn her o!"

"*Aunty Ngozi, warn her o!*"

"I'm serious! I'm not playing!"

"*I'm serious! I'm not playing!*"

"Aunty Ngozi!"

"*Aunty Ngozi!*"

Aunty Ngozi turned on them both. "Ngwa, both of you, leave this kitchen now!"

All afternoon, Chekwube stayed by Soty's side, even when Soty demonstrated her silence by playing on her own and saying no words. She hummed while combing a doll's hair, and Chekwube hummed and combed imaginary hair, more expertly, more believably, as if she were the one with the doll and Soty was grasping air. Chekwube watched as Soty picked a book to read, as she changed TV channels, all the while knowing that Soty's mind was really on her, Chekwube, on holding her silence close so she would give her nothing to mimic. But Chekwube knew how to nurse a grudge, how to feed its embers with images of milk and oil. She imagined Soty and Aunty Ngozi calling her a vagina head behind her back.

Chekwube finessed her craft. The lisp was great, but she could do better; she could make her body do the things that Soty's body did, things that even Soty herself was unaware of. Chekwube widened her eyes to match Soty's dimensions. She put Soty's spring in her steps, adopted her standing and sitting postures so that when Soty looked at Chekwube, she would see a mirror, a mocking, punishing mirror. Chekwube imagined herself as Soty, with the same milk and blood and healing oil flowing inside her. In this role, Chekwube felt she was worthy of the softness that was gifted to Soty. She would partake of Aunty Ngozi's ministrations: the large umbrella, the golden blood of Jesus coating her skin and pouring down her throat. She would choke on blessed Jesus oil.

When Mrs. Onwuchekwa came home and Soty said, "Welcome, Mummy," Chekwube was waiting to pounce.

"Welcome, Mummy."

An oblivious Mrs. Onwuchekwa said thank you to both girls and let Chekwube carry her bag to the dining table, something Soty normally did.

Soty stayed silent the whole evening, answering her mother's attempts at conversation with nods and shakes of the head and frowns and gestures. A puzzled Mrs. Onwuchekwa turned to Aunty Ngozi. "Why isn't she talking?"

"They're playing a game," Aunty Ngozi said.

Chekwube was playing to win.

They were watching *Secrets of Sand* after dinner—Chekwube had found the pizza unremarkable—and when Raquel revealed in the climax of the episode that she was really Raquel pretending to be her boringly good twin sister, Ruth, Soty jumped and pointed at the TV. "Mummy, it's Raquel, I knew it I knew it!"

In the seconds after her outburst, Soty glanced over at Chekwube, her face wracked first with uncertainty, and then with pleading.

"Mummy, it's Raquel, I knew it I knew it!"

Soty ran to her room, slamming the door behind her. Mrs. Onwuchekwa looked from Soty's disappearing figure to Chekwube, who gave an innocent shrug, to Aunty Ngozi, whose eyes were fixed on the TV.

"Ngozi, what kind of game did you say these children are playing?"

Chekwube hid her smile. Soty zero, Bush Girl one hundred million billion.

· · ·

IT WAS THE FIRST DAY of the long holidays, and the girls had no homework or studying to do. Aunty Ngozi was in the kitchen extracting milk from coconuts. The sky was turning gray outside, filling the living room with shadows. Soon, NEPA would cut off the electricity, as happened every time it rained. Chekwube gazed out at the gathering clouds with longing. Since the eating of the ebelebo fruit, the girls had been unable to sneak outside. Aunty Ngozi appeared behind them like a vengeful spirit each time they tried. But Chekwube knew that when the rain began, the downpour would be loud enough to mask the noise of their exit. When the first raindrops crashed against the roof, she leapt from Soty's bed.

"We're going outside," Chekwube said.

"But it's raining," Soty said. Chekwube pouted and wore her pinched look, readying herself to mimic Soty. She noticed Soty flinch as she recognized what Chekwube was about to do. Chekwube relented.

Even though she hadn't been truly sorry, Chekwube had apologized that night after she'd made Soty cry. They'd hugged in Soty's soft bed and confirmed they were still best friends. They'd fallen asleep together. And, as the weeks passed, Chekwube had pretended not to notice when Soty stopped herself mid-sentence to glance at Chekwube, her shoulders tense, eyes wary, waiting for Chekwube to mimic her again. The truth was, Chekwube delighted in Soty's new insecurity. Every once in a while, she would poke at the scab that the *peet-sah* day fight had left: one time when Aunty Ngozi asked for help pounding crayfish and Soty squealed, "Not me, not me," Chekwube at once repeated Soty's words, only offering a belated, unconvincing reassurance to Soty when Soty stared at her like a hurt puppy. "I'm not copying you," Chekwube said, "I'm just talking on my own." These petty tortures were not enough to break Soty, just enough to remind her of the possibility. And Soty was being nicer to her now, even offering her sips from her milk when Aunty Ngozi wasn't watching. Chekwube liked to think she had made their friendship stronger.

"Okay, chicken," Chekwube said, "you can stay here. Me, I'm going."

Soty followed.

The girls filled their lungs with the smell of rain. The water came down hard, running down their faces, soaking through their clothes as they chased each other in circles, then opened their mouths and drank from the sky. Soty was the first one to take her T-shirt off. When Soty's shirt hit the ground, Chekwube suddenly felt like hers was sitting too heavy on her torso; she took hers off too, let it slap the wet concrete. Their bodies would not be contained.

Chekwube watched Soty bare her flat chest to the dark sky. When Soty screamed at the heavens, it was a wordless dare, because in that moment there was nothing delicate about her, nothing in her body or spirit that could snap or bend. If she tripped, the earth would rise to catch her. If she chose to fly, the wind would carry her. If she opened wide enough, she could swallow the universe.

Headlights cut through the darkness and, suddenly, Mrs. Onwuchekwa was there, yelling at the girls. They froze as she hurried out of her car. She gripped each girl by a wet ear and ushered them, wincing and dripping, into the apartment.

Chekwube braced herself for more scolding, but inside the apartment Mrs. Onwuchekwa grew quiet, ignoring Soty's whimpering apologies. She hurried into the kitchen and said something to Aunty Ngozi, who rushed out with a kerosene lantern, flecks of grated coconut flesh dotting her forearm. Even though they'd bathed in the afternoon, Aunty Ngozi led them into the green-tiled bathroom again. The bathwater was scalding.

They sat at the dinner table in silence, the lantern casting an orange light on all their faces. With the electricity gone, there was no TV to distract them. The coconut rice was spicy, with specks of red chili peppers and a mild taste of nutmeg. Soty and Chekwube, without speaking, made a game out of who could eat the most spoons of the peppery rice without sucking air or sipping water to cool their tongues.

Soty sneezed. A spoon clattered against ceramic. Everyone said *bless you*. Soty sneezed again and a half-chewed grain of rice shot out from her mouth and pinged against the glass globe of the lantern. The girls hid their laughter in their bellies.

· · ·

CHEKWUBE WOKE TO SOTY MOANING and writhing beside her. The moaning only got louder the more Chekwube tried to comfort Soty. When Soty started crying, Chekwube got out of bed. There was still no electricity, so she felt her way to the door, and then across the living room, which now felt as familiar as hers, to Mrs. Onwuchekwa's bedroom. She only had to knock once before the door flew open and a silhouette of Mrs. Onwuchekwa stood before her like she'd been waiting to be summoned.

"Soty?"

"Yes," Chekwube said.

Mrs. Onwuchekwa disappeared and reemerged with a lit kerosene lantern.

Back in Soty's bedroom, the moans had grown louder. The bedroom door swung open and there was Aunty Ngozi, in her hairnet and a wrapper tied around her chest. Her mouth was an unmoving line. Mrs. Onwuchekwa went to her room and returned with some tablets in her cupped palm, and a glass of water. Soty forced them down and promptly resumed writhing on the bed. Chekwube stood in a corner of the room and watched. It looked as if some malicious spirit had invaded her friend's body. She'd never heard Soty sound like this, and the few times she'd seen her cry—like on the *peet-sah* day—the tears had always dried up quickly. Now, Soty's eyes were closed, as if whatever she was feeling needed all her attention. The hands of Mrs. Onwuchekwa and Aunty Ngozi raced across Soty's limbs and torso, rubbing Mentholatum ointment on knees and elbows and chest until a cloud of menthol hung in the air, stinging Chekwube's eyes.

"Please, boil some water," Mrs. Onwuchekwa said to Aunty Ngozi. "Let me use it to press her joints." Aunty Ngozi walked toward the door, and Mrs. Onwuchekwa added, "Also, bring your oil from my room. It's in the wardrobe."

Aunty Ngozi nodded. If she felt vindicated for her healing oil ministrations, she said nothing. On her way out of the room, her eyes fell on Chekwube and she looked confused for a second, like she'd forgotten Chekwube was there. She beckoned to Chekwube to follow her. They went into the kitchen and Aunty Ngozi lit a second lantern and set a pot of water to boil.

"What's wrong with Soty?" Chekwube asked.

Aunty Ngozi stayed silent a moment too long. "She's having a sickle cell crisis."

Because you made her play in the rain. Because you made her mother take away her oil. Chekwube imagined Aunty Ngozi thinking these words. She waited for Aunty Ngozi to call her small witch again. Soty's blood was on her head.

They went into Mrs. Onwuchekwa's room and found the bottle of olive oil in the wardrobe, next to the stack of books with *Everywoman*. In the dull light of the lantern, the oil didn't shine like Chekwube remembered.

When Chekwube made to follow Aunty Ngozi back into Soty's room, Aunty Ngozi stopped her, gave her the lantern. "Stay in the parlor." Chekwube obeyed. Moments later, Aunty Ngozi returned with a blanket and a pillow so Chekwube could sleep on the couch. Not like she could actually sleep. In the quiet night, there was only the sound of toads croaking, and Soty moaning from the bedroom.

In the months of their friendship, Soty's sickle cell status had faded from Chekwube's mind. She'd come to think of it as a phantom sickness, or if it was real, it was of little consequence, like needing to wear glasses or having malaria. Sure, Soty had missed a day of school here and there for vague maladies that she brushed aside when Chekwube asked, but she wasn't the only one to ever be sick. Chekwube had also grown accustomed to Soty's bouts of tiredness and had come to believe they were her way of avoiding things she didn't want to do. Surely, her "sickle cell" was just a cover for indulgence, an excuse to justify softness. But now, Soty was in pain. Chekwube pictured Mrs. Onwuchekwa's face drooping with the weight of fear and resolve. And Aunty Ngozi, who'd said nothing but who surely now hated her more than ever.

As time passed, Soty's moans became less frequent, the silences between them stretching longer. Chekwube lay down, but she knew she would not sleep. She breathed in the smell of dust from the folds of the couch. Her mouth tasted salty, rough with the dry grit of sleep. She wanted to pee but was afraid to move, as if moving would somehow cause Soty's pain to return. She left the lantern burning, watching the flame dance on the wick. The toads outside sounded too close, like they were crouched at the windows asking to be let in. She imagined them fat and swollen, drunk on rainwater.

When Chekwube finally fell asleep, she dreamt of blood raining down on her, Aunty Ngozi chanting *small witch* from the shelter of her umbrella.

· · ·

CHEKWUBE WOKE TO AUNTY NGOZI tapping her. "Come, let me take you home."

She dressed quietly in Soty's bedroom, which was now empty, the smell of Mentholatum lingering in the air. Mrs. Onwuchekwa had taken her to the hospital, Aunty Ngozi explained. Chekwube gathered her sleepover clothes into a bag and tried not to cry. She wanted to ask Aunty Ngozi a thousand questions, but her guilt sat so heavy in her chest that she couldn't form words.

As they stepped outside, Chekwube saw the discarded clothes from the evening before, wet and clinging to the ground.

· · ·

IT HAD BEEN THREE DAYS since Soty's crisis, and Chekwube was sure her friend was dead. This was why she'd had the same dream every night since she'd left Soty's house—dreams without sound, like the defective CDs her mother bought from hawkers in traffic; dreams in which she was all alone, the apartment and streets emptied of people. It was why Aunty Ngozi still hadn't shown up with Soty like she'd promised when she dropped Chekwube off at home that morning. The Onwuchekwa household was by now weighed down and haloed with grief, haunted by Soty's empty room, which only days ago had pulsed with life, its vibrant purples now faded.

On the fourth morning, Chekwube woke at dawn and listened to the bus conductors summon their passengers from all corners of the earth. She slipped out of bed, changed into shorts and a T-shirt, and started walking to Soty's house. Her mother would know where to look for her. She concentrated on putting one foot in front of the other, blocking out all thought, because every image that knocked at the doors of her mind felt too dark to bear.

She arrived at Soty's apartment, and the chime of the bell brought her out of her self-induced trance. She should leave. Soty was dead, and Chekwube was the last person they wanted to see.

The door opened and Aunty Ngozi appeared in her nightgown and wrapper. She stepped over the threshold and closed the door behind her. She didn't look like she'd been crying, but maybe Aunty Ngozi mourned differently, her silence and the dryness of her eyes its own kind of suffering.

Aunty Ngozi glared at Chekwube. "Soty is still sleeping."

"She's not dead!" Chekwube blurted out.

Chekwube's knees went weak with relief, and suddenly she was crying in Aunty Ngozi's arms, her face buried in the fabric of her wrapper.

"I thought . . . I thought I made her sick and she died," Chekwube wailed, her words muffled in fabric.

Aunty Ngozi held her until her tears started to subside.

"Many things can cause a crisis," Aunty Ngozi said. "Too much cold, too much heat, stress. We can't name one particular thing. It happens."

It was starting to make sense now, the umbrella, the sweater, the milk, the severity of Aunty Ngozi's attentions.

"She has been asking for you," Aunty Ngozi said. "I've been telling her to eat and take her medicine and get strong, so I can bring her to visit you. And she's been finishing her food these days. I told her mum, 'Come and see o, your baby is eating real food.'"

Chekwube felt like it was the first time she'd heard Aunty Ngozi laugh. It was a husky, layered sound, and when it ended, Chekwube wished it had lasted longer, wished she could hold it in her hands.

"By the time you bring her to see me she'll be plump, I won't recognize her," Chekwube said, smiling through the remnants of her tears.

Aunty Ngozi shrugged. "You're here already. Do you want to see her?"

Chekwube nodded so hard she thought her head might roll off her neck. Aunty Ngozi held the door open and Chekwube walked into the living room. Her eyes adjusted to the low light and the furniture started to take shape before her. She hesitated.

"Go ahead," Aunty Ngozi said as she went into the kitchen. "You know the way."

Chekwube took another step, and then she noticed Soty's purple notebook lying on the couch. She picked it up, opened it, and held it close to her face. With the poor light in the room, Chekwube could not quite make out the squiggles, couldn't tell if Soty had done any new Super S drawings. She closed her eyes, buried her face in the pages, and breathed in. Each breath delivered a simple assurance to Chekwube: the sweet smell of ink lingered on the pages, still there, still alive.

THE HARVEST

WHEN COME YE MINISTRIES FIRST OPENED ITS DOORS
on Igoke Street, just a short walk from Alfonso's own church,
Alfonso's wife would, every few days, bring to his ears some
fresh, searing detail about the pastor or the services and watch
his face, waiting for a reaction.

"I heard they share jollof rice to their members every Sunday. Can you imagine?"

"Alfonso, they now have two Sunday services at that church.
Soon they'll start putting canopies in the street for the overflow!"

It was from Inimfon's lips that Alfonso learned that the
pastor of the new church was nicknamed Daddy Too Much,
because he had countless SUVs and an American wife. "They
say the first time the pastor and his wife met, she fell flat on her
face; she couldn't even stand to shake his hand because of the
power of his anointing." After glancing at Alfonso's stony face,
she added, "People will believe anything. Can you imagine?"

But as the months passed, Inimfon's reports slowly gave way
to a silence that was broken only to carry out the necessary
logistics of their daily lives. And so that morning, they were
both quiet as they prepared for church, their separate routines
long established. Alfonso stood before the cracked mirror on
their bedroom wall and considered putting on a jacket and a tie.

It was a cool morning, but he knew that by afternoon, heat and humidity would be clutching at his neck, causing rivers of sweat to flow down his back. He buttoned up his shirt and tucked it into slightly oversized pants that he held up with a peeling belt. When he marched out to his old car holding his King James Bible and sermon notes—today he'd be preaching Part III of his Unlocking Divine Abundance series—Inimfon was already seated in the passenger's side. Alfonso settled in beside her and turned on the engine. He glanced at Inimfon. She was not wincing at the engine's angry rattling like she often did, nor was she dabbing at sweat on her face or fanning her neck with an old church flyer. She did not lean forward to fiddle with the air conditioner, which hadn't worked in years.

Before her reign of silence began, Inimfon had mentioned that if you stepped inside the new church without a jacket, you could catch a fever from the sheer power of the AC. She'd delivered this information on a Sunday six months ago, while she helped set up for service in the assembly hall of the primary school in Obalende, where Alfonso's church met. Standing with arms akimbo, she'd glared up at the lazy ceiling fans that spread warm, dusty air throughout the room. Again, Alfonso said nothing, and after an eternity of stillness, his wife had sighed. Alfonso imagined that sigh as a eulogy for dead dreams, and in that moment the entire weight of his failures came and sat on his shoulders like a yoke. That same Sunday, during the service, Alfonso had found himself announcing the start of a fundraising campaign, the first of its kind for his church, which he said would enable the church to acquire their own worship space. He'd called the campaign "Build Him a House."

Because the campaign had been divinely inspired, and certainly had nothing to do with the new church a few streets away, Alfonso had decided that the forty-two members of his congregation, none of whom were particularly well-off, would somehow be able to raise the millions they'd need to buy land in the Lekki area, where their church was destined to stand. God would work out the details in His mysterious ways. Alfonso had begun tailoring all of his sermons toward the same message—the negative consequences of a tight fist ("If your hand is closed, how can God put anything into it?") and the blessings that came from giving, and giving generously, to God and His causes. "And what greater cause can there be than to . . ." and Alfonso would bellow, "Say it with me!" and the church would say it with him—albeit with less and less enthusiasm each passing Sunday—"Build Him a House!" He'd also begun sending his members multiple text messages each week, with Bible quotes and reminders about God's love for cheerful givers.

Alfonso had pretended not to notice his membership numbers slowly dwindling, refused to acknowledge the empty spaces opening up where bodies used to warm the benches. Each time Inimfon presented him with the attendance numbers after a service, he would say the same thing he always said: "Glory be to God." Last Sunday, after his usual response, she'd asked, quite loudly, "Glory be to God for only seven people?" She didn't wait for an answer, and as she turned away, her words burrowed under his skin.

It didn't help that his calls and texts to members who'd been absent for many Sundays remained unanswered. He was particularly bothered by Brother Ifeanyi, who had given some excuse about needing to prepare for an exam at school. The young man had been consistent with attendance for over a year, and Alfonso considered him a protégé of sorts and sometimes asked his opinion on sermons he was preparing, not because Alfonso needed guidance from a novice, but to make Brother Ifeanyi feel included.

Alfonso eased his car out of its parking spot between the cinder-block fence of the compound and his neighbor's Toyota. As he drove onto the street, his mouth was dry and his stomach cramped up. The last time he'd had only seven people at a Sunday service, he'd been a nervous young man preaching out of a roadside shed in Iyana Ipaja. It occurred to Alfonso that Inimfon's stories about the new church might have been her way of seeking communion, of voicing the shared fears lurking in the corners of their minds. He thought about reaching across to take her hand. He knew what it would feel like now: rough and callused from carrying them both, unlike when they were newlyweds, the light of his dreams still burning bright.

He had married Inimfon eight years ago for her faith in him, for how readily she'd gone to the places he had envisioned. Before they were married, she would sit in his congregation, week after week, and when he shared his prophecies for the future of his ministry, her hallelujahs were the loudest. He'd had no choice but to notice her. Her enthusiasm, the intensity of her gaze on him as he preached, bestowed upon her an alluring quality. Many Sundays, she would stay behind after service to chat, and with time she began to materialize right there with him when he saw himself leading the megachurch of his future, standing tall beside him in low heels and the old brown hat she wore every Sunday.

What had happened instead was that Inimfon, after she'd moved into his one-room face-me-I-face-you in Mushin and bemoaned the single backyard kitchen and fought nine other tenants over the shared bathrooms, decided that Alfonso's income from the church would not sustain them, and neither would the heavenly manna that he prophesied would rain down on them at any moment. When she'd suggested that Alfonso get a job, he pointed out that he already had one. Harvesting the souls of men was full-time work—one could not serve God and mammon, didn't she know? Of course, Alfonso knew that some preachers had businesses or jobs outside of their churches, but he suspected that this, taking one's eye off the work of ministry, was a slow but sure path to corruption. Besides, he had no head for business, and his only qualification was his calling, which he'd dropped out of LAUTECH to answer—a decision he tried never to dwell on. He'd quoted scriptures to Inimfon about ravens bringing food to Elijah, given her sermons on supernatural provision. In the meantime, he'd said, they could make do with eating two small meals a day. The hunger might do their souls some good, sharpen their faith.

But Inimfon's faith had not held. She'd taken a loan from her sister and paid for a shed near Mushin Market, where she cooked and sold food to traders and commuters. When they were not at church, Inimfon was at her shed, chopping and pounding and frying. Whenever Alfonso offered help, like a good husband, she turned him down. "Save your strength for the church," she'd say with a voice that betrayed nothing.

Soon after Inimfon had begun her food business, Alfonso, desperate to match her achievement, had made a list of ten of the biggest churches in Lagos. He would, he'd decided, present these churches with the opportunity to have him guest-preach a sermon. It didn't even have to be during a Sunday service, a weekday one would do. Once those megachurch pastors heard his preaching—he had recorded one of his best sermons and made it into CDs—they would be falling over themselves to host him in their air-conditioned sanctuaries. Preaching at a big church would put his name in people's mouths. They would come to his services at Tender Lights Primary School, Obalende, to seek him out, the old wooden benches, the heat, the mildew spots in the ceiling all hearkening back to a time when preachers of the gospel didn't need the embellishments of cushioned chairs, expensive audiovisual equipment, and one-hundred-member choirs in matching robes.

Alfonso had found that the road to a megachurch pastor's office was narrower than the road to heaven. He was met by assistants with identical crisp suits and touch-screen tablets, who politely informed him of their bosses' impossible schedules. In a few churches, he'd managed to secure hurried meetings with junior pastors who educated him about their ministries' structures and hierarchies and asked stupid questions, like "What Bible school did you attend?" and "Who have you served under?" He crossed his legs and told each of them how he'd received his calling: when he was a university student, the guest preacher at a ministry event had singled him out from the crowd, waved him to the altar, and prophesied that he, Alfonso, would become a great harvester for the kingdom of God. Alfonso watched the pastors' eyes glaze over. They thanked him for his interest and handed him pamphlets about their School of Ministry, their Discipleship Training—whatever they called it. Where was their fancy school of ministry when he was dropping out of LAUTECH to win souls from the streets of Ogbomoso and all the way to Lagos? Where was their discipleship training when he was preaching in taxis and danfos and molues, getting cursed at by weary commuters?

Inimfon had just hired her second server at the eatery when Alfonso saw the newspaper advertisement for the Higher Level International Ministers' Conference. Alfonso hadn't recognized any of the names on the lineup of speakers, but that was okay, better even—these were the people doing God's work without making noise, without trying to appropriate any of the glory for themselves. The registration fee, inclusive of conference materials, meals, and four nights' accommodation in Akure, was expensive, yes, but the service of God demanded sacrifice. Didn't Inimfon want him to fulfill his calling? She'd given him the money, and he'd called her First Lady in the Making, promising that when they broke ground on their church building, he would remind her of this moment.

Instead, Alfonso had returned early from the conference emptied and hollowed out, with a bitter taste in his mouth that would linger for years. The "conference" was more like a trade fair, with ministers hawking their books, recorded sermons, healing oils, and holy waters. All the talk sessions and grass-to-grace testimonies ended with a call to action, to buy something or join something. He'd been expecting a prayer revival, a place where he would be buoyed by a fresh anointing, a new revelation from the Word. Still, Alfonso had stayed, hoping to find something that would make the experience, and Inimfon's investment, worth it. On the third day, a sweaty fellow in a velvet suit sidled up to Alfonso and handed him a card with a name, phone number, and the title *Solutions Supplier* printed in purple ink. When Alfonso asked what exactly he supplied, the man leaned in and whispered, his hot breath fanning Alfonso's neck, "My brother, any healing you want to happen in your church, I can arrange it for you. Blindness, deafness, cripple, craze, even HIV, mò lè hook ẹ up." Alfonso left the conference that day and avoided Inimfon's questions when he got home. He'd told himself there had to be a right way to achieve megachurch status, a godly way, without salesmen and arrangers of miracles. He would pray and fast and wait. Alfonso had a calling, and God would prove Himself in His time.

While Alfonso had waited, Inimfon had acquired more staff and expanded her eatery, upgrading from sand floors to concrete, and from no walls to plywood boards. She replaced squeaky wooden benches with plastic chairs and tables and bought standing fans to cool her customers while they ate. She had less and less energy for his waning prophecies about their future. Her amens and hallelujahs grew weak like old dishwater. And when she prayed, she no longer spent many minutes calling God by all of His names. She deployed her prayers like arrows at a target, as though she expected God to understand she could no longer afford to spend too much time on her knees. Sometimes, Alfonso grew angry on God's behalf, and was tempted to point out that everything she had achieved had come from God and not her own effort or wisdom. But whenever he opened his mouth to rebuke Inimfon, a twinge of doubt would cause him to pause and look around him at the one-bedroom apartment they'd moved into, with its own kitchen and bathroom inside, paid for by Inimfon's sweat, and shame would spread in his chest, taking up so much space that there was little room for breath.

Sometimes, in the early hours of morning when his sleep was interrupted by an inchoate unease, Alfonso wondered whether the reason Inimfon adhered to her strict regimen of daily contraceptives even as their sex life withered was not, as she claimed, because they couldn't afford to care for a child, but because Inimfon was wary of the fleshly bond that a child would represent, the added difficulty of extricating herself from him. But he'd never challenged her on this, afraid to have his suspicions confirmed. The closest he'd come was making a joke once about how they should have children so they could increase the numbers at his church. Inimfon hadn't even cracked a smile.

Alfonso slowed the car and took the exit for Obalende; in a few minutes they would arrive at his church. He tried to remind himself that money and numbers were not the most important things for a minister. He took pride in knowing all the members of his church as individuals, knowing what kept their heads from resting easy at night. He was at his best, his most unimpeachable, when he went on his knees on behalf of his small flock, whether it was to ask God to ease the trouble in the Okories' tumultuous marriage, or to pray for healing for Sister Remi, who had hypertension, or to give thanks with young Faaji, who disappeared every once in a while for weeks on end and resurfaced with a large offering and vague testimonies about God prospering his work. Alfonso was especially protective of Brother Ifeanyi, with his rough edges and overexposure to Ajegunle's hard streets. It had taken some time but Alfonso, with God's help, of course, had slowly tamed Brother Ifeanyi. He no longer turned up in church proudly hungover and showing off the bumps and bruises from his latest fistfight, or spent what little money he had gambling on 247Moni, or wore his ripped jeans so low they exposed the swell and split of his buttocks. Alfonso was proud of his work. The first time he'd met Brother Ifeanyi, the young man had been caught stealing a mobile phone from an electronics store where Alfonso had gone to hand out his church flyers. The shop owner was holding on to Brother Ifeanyi's shirt collar with one hand, brandishing her phone with the other as she threatened to call the police and have him locked up for life. Only Alfonso's pleas, delivered on his knees along with Brother Ifeanyi's, and his promise to personally see to the young man's rehabilitation, had convinced the shop owner to let Brother Ifeanyi go. From that day on, Alfonso had taken responsibility for Brother Ifeanyi, making sure he stopped skipping his lectures at Yaba Tech, and that he cut all ties with the girl with whom he'd been fornicating, the same girl he'd been trying to impress with the phone he'd attempted to steal.

But now, Alfonso worried that his work might be coming undone, given Brother Ifeanyi's long absence. Without Alfonso's influence, it would be too easy for the young man to slide back into his self-destructive ways.

"Brother Ifeanyi hasn't been answering my calls," Alfonso said to Inimfon, without looking away from the road.

She shrugged. "People are busy these days."

"Too busy to come to church or send a text message?" Alfonso said. "No, no, he needs to do better. If he's absent again today, I'll go and visit him after service."

Inimfon said nothing.

. . .

ALFONSO PARKED IN FRONT OF the two-story building that housed Tender Lights Primary School. When he'd approached the headmaster about using the school's assembly hall for his church services, he'd meant for it to be only a temporary arrangement. Now, a decade later, Alfonso walked to the school gates with heavy feet, Inimfon's shadow falling across him and partially shielding him from the sun. The school building, with its ash-gray walls grimy from children's fingers, and windows hanging askew from their frames, had become too familiar. Even with his eyes closed, he'd know how to avoid the broken bits of concrete ground within the compound that collected rainwater, how to position himself behind the lectern, to hold it just so because too much weight would cause it to lean to the right.

Alfonso pushed open the gate and knocked on the wall of the plywood shack beside it. The door creaked open and a hand held out the key to the assembly hall, the school's gateman not needing visual confirmation of Alfonso's presence after the clattering of his car's engine. They walked to the assembly hall, Alfonso wondering if Inimfon felt the same weight that he did pushing down on him. He stopped outside the hall, key in hand, but made no move to open the door. He could hear the unasked question forming on Inimfon's lips. He held out the key to her.

"Start setting up. I'll be back."

She took the key with a puzzled frown. "Where are you going?"

Alfonso hurried out through the school gate, fleeing his wife's gaze.

. . .

ALFONSO TURNED LEFT AT THE END of Ferguson Road. The streets were peaceful, as they tended to be this early on a Sunday morning. It had rained in the night, but the air was losing its coolness as the sun rose higher, bathing tired old buildings in a surreal light. Alfonso could almost ignore the FanYogo and Gala wrappers and the Power Horse cans that littered the street and clogged the roadside gutters. The abandoned vehicles on the side of the road, long ago stripped of their doors and fixtures, faded into soft colors on the edge of his vision.

It felt like ages ago that he'd first come across the demolition on Igoke Street. With his car at the mechanic's, he'd taken a danfo that carried him past the site. When he noticed the empty skyline where a cluster of old apartment buildings used to stand, he played a guessing game with himself, wondering what would be erected once the rubble was cleared away. It left him with a strange melancholia; a feeling that, like these buildings, his entire being could be wrecking-balled out of existence with a single stroke. He knew the day would come when whatever structure arose in place of the fallen ones would feel like it had always stood there, everything so utterly replaceable.

Alfonso hesitated as he approached Igoke Street. He thought about turning around, retracing his steps back to Ferguson and the safety of Tender Lights. But there was something more menacing about the spectre of the unseen.

As Alfonso neared the former demolition site, he could make out a white, dome-shaped structure and, the closer he got, the larger it loomed. Beside the dome stood a billboard with the smiling faces of Apostle Goodwill O. Ofobrukueta (aka Daddy Too Much) and First Lady Lois Ofobrukueta, her lips a slash of red, gold jewelry dangling from her ears, and blond hair framing a pale face. Alfonso had been prepared for this Daddy Too Much to have Jheri-curled hair down to his shoulders and a shiny robe—a ridiculous picture to go with his nickname. But this was a face stellar in its ordinariness, with a neatly trimmed beard and a low haircut. The apostle was dressed in a white suit that matched his wife's. Alfonso forced his feet to carry him forward, toward the dome, until he was standing before a high white wall with the words Come Ye Global Ministries embossed onto it in gold letters.

Alfonso swallowed past the dryness in his mouth and headed for the gates. He pushed on the pedestrian entrance, not truly believing that such an imposing thing would succumb to his touch. The gate swung open silently to reveal ground paved with interlocking concrete tiles in gray and maroon. The dome turned out to be an enormous freestanding marquee reinforced with glass and steel. At the top of the marquee's entrance, Daddy Too Much and his wife stared down from a large banner, both of them wearing bright smiles, the words *Welcome Home* printed across their torsos in triumphant font.

Voices seemed to be coming from inside the marquee. This early, the only people in church would be workers and volunteers helping to set up, and perhaps some of the church's leaders. Alfonso followed the voices.

As soon as he stepped inside the dome, goose pimples studded his skin. Along the walls, large floor-standing air conditioners spewed clouds of freezing air. Elaborate chandeliers made of glass and gold and crystal, and swaths of silky fabric, hung from the ceiling, hiding what he imagined would be the bars and bolts that held up the roof. The room was divided in half by a red carpet that ran all the way to an altar, where tall vases stood bursting with flowers. The altar also featured a shiny pulpit made of polished glass and, behind it, a row of overstuffed armchairs in red and gold upholstery. Yet another banner, this one behind the altar, displayed an image of the Apostle and his First Lady in matching outfits.

The room bustled with activity—a small group of people held hands, bouncing on their feet and shouting prayers up toward heaven. Others were covering the chairs for the congregation with protective fabric. Young women in high heels, blazers that looked sharp enough to cut glass, and long hair extensions that swayed with their every step floated between the rows, placing bulletins and offering envelopes on the seats. Alfonso shook his head. Of course, these were the kinds of people who would be drawn to a church like this: sharp dressers, attractive to the eye but empty on the inside. All shine, no substance.

Alfonso felt a hand on his arm. He looked up at the face of its owner, and his mouth fell open. Brother Ifeanyi glanced around the room before guiding Alfonso toward the exit. Outside the marquee, Brother Ifeanyi avoided Alfonso's eyes. Alfonso assessed the man before him, top to bottom. He looked like an entirely new person in shiny black shoes, dress pants, and a navy-blue blazer.

Alfonso's eye was drawn to the tag hanging from a lanyard around Brother Ifeanyi's neck.

"You're an usher? When did you start coming here?" Alfonso asked.

Before Brother Ifeanyi could respond, the pedestrian gate swung open and a woman walked in. As she passed them, Alfonso locked eyes with her for a second before she looked away.

"Sister Boma!" Alfonso called out. Sister Boma quickened her steps and disappeared into the freezing marquee. Alfonso spun back to Brother Ifeanyi. "How many of you are here?"

"Just me and Sister Boma," Brother Ifeanyi said, still not looking at Alfonso.

Alfonso didn't know whether to believe him. He could be lying to end the conversation quickly, to get him to leave. But that wasn't about to happen. Brother Ifeanyi, more than any other member of his church, owed him an explanation.

"I can understand if the others just leave like that. But you, ehn, Ifeanyi?"

Brother Ifeanyi stared at a spot on Alfonso's right shoulder. "Pastor Al, I'm finishing school next year, and things are hard. Is there anybody in your church that can give me a good job after I graduate?"

"Have you forgotten that if not for me, you'd be graduating inside prison?"

Alfonso regretted the words as soon as he said them. Still, the image of Brother Ifeanyi on the day they'd first met, the boy in torn jeans and a ragged T-shirt, on his knees begging to be rescued, was sharp in his memory. Never mind the sleek clothes he was now sporting, a pathetic future had awaited the boy before Alfonso's intervention. It was Alfonso who deserved an apology.

Brother Ifeanyi broke the silence. "I can never forget how you helped me. But, Pastor Al, I need something different now."

"Yes, you need connections, right?" Alfonso sneered. "You need fraudsters like your Daddy Too Much who sell miracles and blessings, and suck people dry. But I don't blame them; I blame their followers, people like you. All you people care about is money and glory."

Brother Ifeanyi's mirthless laughter caught Alfonso by surprise. "What about you? Every single Sunday with your Build Me a House."

"It's Build *Him* a House!"

"Whatever," Brother Ifeanyi said. His dismissive tone grated on Alfonso, caused his face to burn with anger. "But since everybody is building houses, who should I listen to? You, or the man of God that built this place and filled it up, times two, in a year?"

"That's what you have to say to me?" Alfonso said, his voice rising. "After I treated you like a son, after everything I—"

Brother Ifeanyi looked around him, like he was embarrassed to be anywhere near Alfonso. "Pastor Al, please, I have work to do. Our first service is starting soon."

Brother Ifeanyi hurried away, and Alfonso thought about running after him, ripping that lanyard from his neck, stuffing it down his throat. But the protective heat of his anger was already fading, leaving him colder than when he'd walked into the dome. He fumbled for his collar and undid the top button, but the tightness in his throat persisted. He felt foolish, standing there by himself like an abandoned lover, and so he forced his feet to move toward the gate.

Outside the church compound, Alfonso's eyes drifted upward to the billboard with the Apostle and his First Lady. He imagined Daddy Too Much preaching a powerful sermon to Alfonso's own congregation against being unequally yoked with failure: "Your God is not poor, so why should your pastor be? How can you be guided to prosperity by a pauper?" He saw his members' brows furrow in concentration, heads nodding along, mouths amening in holy agreement. He saw Inimfon in that congregation, freshly enlightened, in a new church hat with ornate feathers that reached for the heavens.

·   ·   ·

INIMFON WAS WIPING THE LECTERN with a rag. She spared Alfonso only a glance as he appeared in the doorway, but how he must look to her, the complete opposite of the dreams he'd sold her.

On his walk back to Tender Lights he'd mulled over Brother Ifeanyi's words. "Build Me a House," Brother Ifeanyi had said. A mistake, or a pointed accusation? Alfonso had become unrecognizable to himself. Maybe the visiting preacher's prophecy all those years ago was a lie, mere theatrics. Or maybe Alfonso would indeed do great things, but they would not be projected from massive screens strategically positioned in a freezing church building the size of a football stadium. Maybe he was made for fellowship with a small community where he knew the people by name and could nurture their individual gifts, where they weren't a massive faceless crowd. Could he win back his runaway congregation? And Inimfon. If he put a new vision on the table, would she stay?

Alfonso took another step into the assembly hall, toward Inimfon. He didn't know how to form the words he knew he should say to her, and so he tried to form his body, the entirety of his being, into a penance—for the smell of dust in the air, the thick cobwebs hanging high up in the ceiling, the cement floor whose shine had long died, for Inimfon's secondhand gray skirt suit and the battered hat she'd worn every Sunday since she first walked through those very doors. Alfonso knew he could never be like the Daddy Too Muches of this world—he'd never been the kind of man who could go to America and pluck a wife like she had been cultivated just for him, and he would never be the kind of preacher who would amass the power to bulldoze long-standing structures so he could have a place. He had to tell Inimfon this, tell her something. But they had a service to prepare for. He found a second rag and proceeded to wipe benches.

. . .

WHEN IT WAS 8:00 AM, Alfonso positioned himself behind the lectern and waited for the door to swing open. After a few minutes, tired of standing still, he began pacing the length of the hall, and did so for the entire thirty minutes of Sunday school while Inimfon sat quietly. Nobody showed up. Alfonso reminded himself that it was not uncommon for members to skip Sunday school and turn up only for the main service. But by 9:20 it was still just him and Inimfon in the room.

The silence stretched on for so long, Alfonso thought it would snap. "We should start the service," he said. "The Bible says that where two or three are gathered in His name . . ."

Inimfon shook her head. "Alfonso, there's nobody here."

Alfonso stepped away from the lectern and joined Inimfon on the bench where she sat. It creaked under their combined weight.

"I went to see that new church," Alfonso said, without looking at Inimfon. "Sister Boma was there . . . Brother Ifeanyi."

"I've been trying to tell you."

This was the time to acknowledge all the things she'd been trying to tell him, and to tell her the things he needed to say, things he needed to repent for—his silences and resentments, the shadow that his pride and ego had cast over their lives.

When he finally opened his mouth, it was to make a flaccid joke, one rendered sour by its proximity to truth. "Maybe I should come and be a serving boy at your restaurant"—he gave a weak laugh—"since I don't have members anymore." He hoped Inimfon would smile, respond with a counter-joke, and then some reassurance, something blandly benign, like "It is well" or "God is in control." Her answer was a noncommittal "Hmm."

Alfonso wondered why it was so much easier to talk to an unseen God than to the person beside him, made of flesh and blood, like him. But people were capricious, and prayer was a shield. He would ask God to soften Inimfon, make her recognize his essential goodness and the repentance in his heart, without him having to grovel or debase himself before her. Alfonso bowed his head and closed his eyes. He didn't move when he felt the air shift beside him, but his heart sang with gratitude; Inimfon was getting on her knees to join him in prayer.

Alfonso heard the door creak, and when he opened his eyes he was alone. He found Inimfon minutes later, seated in the car, her hat tossed to the floor of the back seat. He got in beside her and turned the key in the ignition, filling the space between them with shaking.

EDEN

· ·

MADU HAD NEVER REACHED INTO THE BACK OF THE
videocassette cupboard: that dark, dusty place where the films
were older than God. But today, bored and desperate not to
rewatch another movie—they'd already watched *Living in
Bondage*, *Terminator 2*, and *Mortal Kombat* many times over—he
got on his knees and thrust his hand into the cupboard, taking
out the first tape he touched. The cassette had his father's initials on its side, written in black ink on a strip of adhesive paper.

His sister, Ifechi, peered at it. "What film is that?"

Holding the cassette up to his face, Madu read the title: "*A
Taste of Paradise.*"

Ifechi hesitated. "Madu . . . it's Daddy's film."

"So what?"

Madu stood and took the tape out of its case, noticing,
through the clear plastic in the cassette's center, that both spools
had an almost equal amount of tape around them. He slipped
the tape into the videocassette player and pressed *play*. The
familiar whirring sound started up from the cassette player. A
penis filled the screen.

"Jesus!" Madu shrieked, jumping back and away from the
TV without taking his eyes off it. His sister stared at the screen
like it had suddenly grown fangs. For a while, the only sounds

in the living room were the hum of the cassette player and the creaking of the ceiling fan as the blades turned. The old TV was acting up again—there was no sound. Madu crept toward the TV and brought his palm down against its side twice, sharply, like he'd seen their father do many times. It worked. They heard moaning sounds carried on waves of jazzy background music.

A man and a woman, both with pale skin and blond hair, a white bed, white walls, a white floor littered with long-stemmed red roses, all the more stark against all that white. The woman lay on the bed, smiling, her legs spread so wide she looked two-dimensional. Ifechi, distressed to find that the exposed flesh between the woman's legs was the same pink as her favorite pinafore, decided that yellow was her new color. The man straddled the woman's head.

"She's eating it sha!" Madu said, his mouth hanging open on the "sha."

Ifechi glanced at the front door. "Madu, what if Aunty Hope comes?"

Aunty Hope ran the hair salon downstairs, and she looked in on Madu and Ifechi while their parents were at work. It was also her job to make sure they didn't mix with the "urchins," as their father liked to call the happy, unkempt bunch that ran about the neighborhood in packs most afternoons, rolling old motorcycle tires down the potholed streets.

With the children on holidays, Aunty Hope had to check on them more often. Some days she would take them down to her salon and make them sit, with their books, on her brown couch whose cushions had sunk into craters from decades of use. The salon was a small room with a faded blue-and-white-checkered floor and a sweet chemical smell. One wall was mostly taken up by a cracked mirror where Aunty Hope's customers would stand preening and, sometimes, complaining about a section of hair that had not set properly in the curlers, or Aunty Hope's miserly use of Lottabody. In one corner of the salon, there was a hair-washing sink that stood on three legs, and an armless plastic chair that used to be white. Because the shop had no plumbing, a large bucket was positioned under the hair-washing sink, with a short hose that connected the bottom of the sink to the bucket. Aunty Hope always let the bucket get dangerously full before she, with a heavy sigh, would slowly drag it from beneath the sink and carry it, with bent back, to the gutter in front of the compound, where the murky bucket water joined the rest of the neighborhood's liquid waste.

Madu and Ifechi had learned how to deal with Aunty Hope. Her moods were tied to the frequent and unannounced NEPA power cuts: happy when there was power, surly otherwise. Like many of the residents and small businesses in their Obalende neighborhood, Aunty Hope could not afford a generator. Sometimes Aunty Hope would invite the children to "come and learn" her work. Ifechi particularly liked watching her comb creamy white relaxer into the women's hair. She liked the acrid smell of it and felt a malicious delight when the women scrunched up their faces as it started to burn their scalps. At seven, Ifechi was not allowed to have her hair relaxed. She longed to turn ten, like Madu. She would be a big girl then.

"Go and lock the front door," Madu said, still looking at the TV. Ifechi stayed put, frowning and shuffling her feet. Madu turned around to face her. "Ifechi, go and lock the door!"

Ifechi stomped to the front door, locked it, and returned to her place, her brother's glare following her.

Ifechi was finding it hard to breathe. The room got warmer, the air thicker, as minutes passed. The woman was on her hands and knees now, the man behind her. They both looked like they were in pain.

"I don't want to watch anymore," Ifechi said, her voice hoarse with unshed tears.

"Then stop watching," Madu said. "Silly baby."

Ifechi swallowed. She did not turn away.

. . .

UNCLE ZUBBY AND AUNTY AGODI lived on Glover Road in Ikoyi, in a big white house enclosed by a tall fence topped with barbed wire. A large Beware of Dogs sign, with a drawing of a growling rottweiler that didn't exist, hung from the solid black gate. Even though their family lived only a few minutes away, in Obalende, Madu and Ifechi's parents were careful not to visit too often. "Before they start to think we only visit for their light and AC," their mother would say, with a sharp edge to her voice.

Madu and Ifechi enjoyed visiting Uncle Zubby and Aunty Agodi. They would pile into the Santana and ride with the windows down, warm breeze and exhaust smoke blowing in their faces. They would look out the window as they passed the familiar sights: the police barracks with faded gray walls and roof sheets flapping in the wind; the small market on the edge of their street where tomato and cabbage pyramids stood wilting in the sun, butchers letting large green-and-blue flies run giddy on blood and entrails. On Ikoyi Road, they would pass the hulking buildings in the old Federal Secretariat complex, with almond trees dotting the grounds. It was around this point that the noise and muck of Obalende began to give way to Ikoyi's genteel influence. The streets grew quieter. Colonial-style houses stood proud in vast, tree-lined compounds with green lawns. Even the air felt different, lighter, like you could fly if you breathed in enough of it. The children would often spot white people in shorts and sandals walking exotic-looking dogs, and they would stare at the dog-walkers until they became flecks in the distance.

Madu didn't mind that Uncle Zubby and Aunty Agodi had no children for him and Ifechi to play with, even though his mother often said how unfortunate this was. For Madu, it was enough that they always had electricity at their house, their big generator standing in when NEPA failed. Plus, his uncle had loads of video games, and comic books that he let Madu borrow and not return. Ifechi liked Aunty Agodi—she made the best chin chin in the world!—but she liked Uncle Zubby more. He reminded her of Father Christmas, with his lips buried beneath a forest of graying beard. Every time the beard parted to let him speak, Ifechi would feign surprise to find his lips there. Uncle Zubby always greeted her with a hug, and Ifechi would raise her forehead and rub her skin against the crisp hairs on his chin.

On this visit, the adults sent Madu and Ifechi into the smaller living room upstairs—the one with the fuzzy center rug that Ifechi liked—with soft drinks, a platter of chin chin, and the TV while they sat and talked in the larger one on the ground floor. Ifechi sipped her Fanta and wished her brother would settle on a channel; he'd been fiddling with the TV remote since they got there. She didn't see why they couldn't watch *Matilda* or *Pingu*.

She listened to the laughter of the adults drifting up from the downstairs living room and tried to make out their words. She remembered the conversation she'd overheard last week.

"Madu."

"What?"

"Come closer, let me tell you something," Ifechi said, glancing at the doorway to make sure nobody was coming.

"You come here," Madu said as he changed channels again. Ifechi sighed and shuffled closer to her brother on the couch.

"Do you know," Ifechi started, her voice low, "that when a girl becomes a big girl, if a boy touches her she will get pregnant?"

Madu stared at Ifechi in reproving silence.

"Just touch like this o," Ifechi said, poking her brother's thigh to demonstrate.

"You're stupid."

"But it's true! I heard Mummy and Clementina's mummy saying it. Remember last Sunday when Clementina's mummy came after church. When I went to the kitchen to get water, I heard them. They didn't see me, but I heard them."

Madu found a channel showing a He-Man and She-Ra cartoon. He placed the remote beside him on the couch. "So you're an eavesdropper," he said.

"What's 'eavesdropper'?"

"Olodo, don't they teach you English in primary three?"

"You're abusing me, abi?" Ifechi said. "Okay, I won't tell you anything again." She sat back with a pout, her hands folded across her chest.

"Okay, sorry," Madu said. "Sorry. Tell me."

Ifechi's face lit up as she turned to her brother again. "They were saying that one of their friends' daughters got pregnant. They said all the boys in Lagos have touched her, that's why they don't now know which one is the father."

"Oh, so you mean if I touch you now, you will get pregnant?" Madu asked, laughing as he touched Ifechi's neck. "I've touched you; now you're pregnant."

"No jor," Ifechi said, frowning at her brother's show of ignorance. "They said it's when somebody is a big girl. I'm not a big girl yet."

"And how will you know when you become a big girl?"

Ifechi glanced at the doorway again. "You didn't hear what Clementina's mummy said. She said that Clementina . . . that blood was coming out of Clementina's pee-pee. That means she is now a big girl. If you see her in school when we resume, better don't touch her."

"Why are you lying, Ifechi? How can a person pee blood?"

"Shhhh! I'm not lying; that's what they said. Clementina's mummy said she told Clementina that if a boy touches her, she will become pregnant. And Mummy said she will tell me the same thing too when I'm a big girl."

"So where does the blood come from? Will there be a wound inside your tummy?"

"Me, I don't know, but that's what they said."

Madu contemplated this for a moment. "So after you start peeing blood, if I touch you, you will get pregnant?"

Ifechi blinked up at the ceiling and considered the question. "No," she decided. "Because you're my brother. If it's another boy, then I will get pregnant. Then my tummy will swell like a watermelon and my pee-pee will tear when the baby is coming out."

"Ifechi!"

"But that's what they said; it's not me that said it!"

Madu rolled his eyes and turned to the TV. But he was curious and so, even though he hadn't decided if he believed his sister, he asked, "What if a boy touches you by mistake? Just by mistake o."

"I will still get pregnant," Ifechi said with quiet certainty. "That means that once I become a big girl, I won't allow any boy to come near me. And you too, don't be touching girls anyhow." Ifechi pulled her earlobe for emphasis. "Because you can't know who is big."

Madu frowned. "How do I know you're even telling the truth?" he asked.

Ifechi shrugged. "I've told you. If you like, don't hear. Mummy said that if any of her children disgrace her, she will send us back to our father in heaven."

They watched the TV in silence for a few minutes.

"Madu."

"What?"

"Will Mummy send us to heaven if they catch us watching those bad films?"

Madu reached for a handful of chin chin and stuffed it in his mouth.

· · ·

ONE RAINY NIGHT WHEN THERE was no electricity, the children played Catch the Light with their father. Their mother lay on the couch, laughing and shouting warnings—"Careful, watch her head!" Catch the Light was their game, invented by their father for nights like this, when electricity was gone and stomachs were full and the silence in the room had no extra weight to it. He would put out the candles and let the warm darkness surround them. Then he would turn on his flashlight and move the beam of light on the floor and all around the room, the children scrambling to touch it with their hands or feet. It was the only game they played together.

The stakes were high on this night. Their father had promised the winner three over-the-head spins, to be redeemed at any time of the winner's choosing. Madu and Ifechi loved being held above the head of their tall father, loved opening their eyes to see the furniture, barely discernible in the dark, whirling around them. A dizzying sensation remained after they were set down gently, like honey lingering on their tongues. But most of all they loved the chafing feel of their father's palms as he gripped them, and they imagined that his hands left an imprint that remained long after he let go.

The children rushed from spot to spot, shrieking and stretching their limbs toward the light. But just when they thought they'd got it, the light would move away and they would laugh out their frustration. The light was all they could see, and they followed wherever it went, sometimes bumping into each other and their father.

One time, their father directed the beam of light to a spot close to his feet. Ifechi followed, but instead of chasing the light, her eyes landed on her father's right foot. The nail of his big toe was long, yellow from the light, specks of dirt or lint stuck in the corners where nail met skin. Ifechi could not move. In one of her father's films, a man had moaned in ecstasy while he kissed and nibbled on a woman's foot, sucked on the dainty toes with their red nail polish, opened his mouth wide as half of the woman's foot vanished into it.

Ifechi felt her heart pounding as she pulled her eyes away from her father's foot. She glanced at her mother's dark form on the couch. Had her mother's feet ever disappeared into the mouth of her father like that, like prey being consumed by a python? Had her father made sounds just like the man in the film, like he was dying but didn't want it to stop? Ifechi tried to find her father's face in the gloom, certain that he knew what she was thinking, what she and Madu had done. But he was still moving the light, and Madu was still running and screaming. Everything felt normal.

When their father was ready to let someone win, it was Madu who was chosen. Madu and their father spun together, their laughter filling the empty spaces in the room, while Ifechi watched with remorse from her place on the ground.

. . .

MADU'S DREAMS HAD STARTED ABOUT a week after he
and Ifechi watched the first of their father's films. Dreams
of lush pubic hairs in rainbow colors and breasts with dusky,
hard-looking peaks that surely tasted like cola candy. Madu had
considered telling Ifechi about the dreams, how they left his
mouth dry and his heart thumping. But how would she help; all
she knew how to do was cry. Madu did not consider telling his
parents: his father would send for his koboko, and his mother
would make him kneel with his hands raised for hours and then
command him to fill a twenty-leaf notebook with the words "I
will not be a bad boy in Jesus's name" in capital letters.

In this latest dream, a woman looked up from the penis
she'd been painting with her tongue, turned in his direction,
and stared into his soul. She smiled and beckoned with an index
finger. Madu woke up to find his penis straining against his
pajama bottoms. He glanced at Ifechi's bed across from his. Satisfied that she was asleep, he felt the unfamiliar hardness with
a tentative hand, awe and dread churning inside him. When
Madu noticed that it felt good touching himself, he shoved his
hands under his pillow, squeezing his eyes shut as he murmured
Hail Marys. After twenty slow recitals, Madu's penis went back
to normal.

He let out a sigh and slept like the innocent.

. . .

MADU AND IFECHI WERE WATCHING *Pussy Palace* one
afternoon—with their parents at work, the front door locked,
and Aunty Hope busy in her salon—when the TV screen went

dead. Like people emerging from a cave into daylight, the children squinted all around them: at the pale green walls; at the family photo on the shelf above the TV; at the tiny rabbit family that shared the shelf space, *Made in Taiwan*, blameless and perfect in matching red dungarees; at the Jesus with sad eyes staring love and guilt at them from the wall across the room. In the vacuum left behind by the now-silent appliances, they could hear the cry of the Agege bread hawker outside, the honk of the newspaper vendor's horn, a baby crying next door. The ceiling fan slowed to a stop above their heads.

"Don't worry," Madu said, as much for his own comfort as for his sister's. "NEPA will bring back the light before Mummy and Daddy come back . . . Don't worry . . ."

The hours passed and the electricity did not return. The tape player stayed silent and stoic as Madu prodded it with angry fingers, pushing the eject button over and over, lifting the player up from its stand, turning it upside down, as though to coax it into spitting out the cassette.

"Hei, God . . ." Ifechi prayed-sang every few minutes, trying not to cry because she knew it would annoy Madu. "Please, let NEPA bring back the light before Mummy and Daddy come." But by six thirty, when their parents returned, all the praying and glaring had neither restored the electricity nor caused the cassette to eject itself from the machine.

All evening, Madu and Ifechi tiptoed around their mother while she made dinner in the hot kitchen. Sweat formed on their brows. They offered their help with sweet smiles. They worried their mother with questions, which she answered with a slightly tortured air while stirring stew on the kerosene stove. Eventually, she waved them out of the kitchen with her ladle.

As the family sat down to eat, Madu and Ifechi exchanged nervous glances. When their father cleared his throat to say grace, they lowered their eyelids but kept their eyes open, watching the candlelight play on their parents' faces.

The children picked at their dinner of boiled yams and stew with much ceremony, unable to taste anything, not even that smoky aftertaste of kerosene that seemed to flavor all their meals. They made their cutlery clink busily against the ceramic plates, but their mother wasn't fooled.

"Why aren't you two eating?" she asked.

"We're full," Ifechi said.

"Full? You've not even eaten anything." Their mother frowned as she reached forward and felt their necks, Madu's first, then Ifechi's, with the back of her hand. "Are you not feeling well?"

"We're well, Mummy," they chorused. Not feeling well meant visits to the hospital, and injections. They shoveled in the food.

Without warning, the joyful symphony of working appliances started up in the house again. The ceiling fan began to turn, sending the flames from the candles into a mad dance. The children sat very still while their mother stood, with a grateful sigh, to close the drapes, blow out the candles, and turn on the lights.

After dinner, their father settled down in front of the TV for the evening news while their mother did the dishes. Madu and Ifechi stayed in the living room with their father long after their mother had gone to bed, watching over the tape player and the evidence inside it, pretending to be taken with the NTA documentary about cassava farming that was showing. It was only a matter of time before their father would get up to go to the toilet, or to get something out of his room.

After the documentary, their father looked at Madu and Ifechi, as though noticing their presence for the first time since dinner.

"It's almost ten," he said. "You two go to bed."

"But we're not feeling sleepy yet," Ifechi said.

"And school is still on break," Madu added.

"Did I say this was a debate?" their father said, leaning forward in his chair. The children got up and shuffled out of the living room. They hid in the doorway, peeping at their father. Without turning his head, their father called out, "Madu, Ifechi, if I come out and find you still standing there ehn . . ."

The children ran into their bedroom and lay down in silence, listening for sounds from the living room. They thought they heard their father moving about and hoped he was going to bed.

"What if Daddy—" Ifechi whispered.

"Shhh!"

They lay quiet for what felt like a very long time. Madu stared at the water stain on the ceiling above his bed like it could save him, and Ifechi began to drift off into a restless slumber. But the next sound wiped every trace of sleep from her eyes and almost stopped her brother's heart.

"Madu! Ifechi!"

Ifechi felt a dribble of hot liquid seep between her legs. She clamped her thighs together. "Madu! Daddy is calling us," she said.

"Shut up," Madu hissed. "Do as if you're sleeping."

"Madu! Ifechi! Come out here now!" Their father's voice was closer. They could hear his footsteps approaching their door.

"Madu," Ifechi moaned.

"Shut up," Madu said. "Don't say anything."

The children's bedroom door flew open. Their father filled the doorway.

"Both of you, get up right now!" he said.

Madu blinked up at his father's face. "Yes, Daddy?" he said, attempting a sleepy murmur. Ifechi, with her wide eyes, was less convincing.

"Get out now! To the parlor!" their father said.

They stumbled out of their beds as their mother came to the door. "Chuma," she said to their father. "What is it?"

Their father gave no reply. He followed behind Madu and Ifechi as they staggered into the living room. Their mother joined them seconds later.

"Who has been watching this film?" their father said, brandishing the cassette tape.

Ifechi glanced up from her feet to her brother's face. Maybe if she confessed quickly, their father would have mercy. She could tell the truth and shame the devil. She could say it was Madu's idea. Which was the truth.

"What film is that? Let me see," their mother said. She stepped closer and took the tape from their father. She read the title, and her body grew tense. She gave her husband a long, pointed glare as she held out the cassette to him. He took it without looking at her face. She turned to Madu and Ifechi.

"So I have been breeding dirty maggots in this house, ehn?" she said. "Instead of reading your books, this is what you spend your time doing when we are at work."

"This is the last time I will ask both of you," their father said. "Who watched this film?"

Ifechi looked at the tape in her father's hand. His palm now covered the portion of paper on the cassette that had his initials.

"It was me."

Ifechi snapped her head up to look at her brother. He was staring into the space in front of him, like he was seeing things nobody else could.

"Only you, Madu?" their father asked, after a brief silence. He turned to Ifechi. "What about you?"

"She was with Aunty Hope," Madu said.

"Is that true?" their mother asked Ifechi, who could only nod.

"Ifechi, go to my room and bring my koboko," their father said.

Ifechi managed to steady her legs and direct them out of the living room and down the dim corridor. The floor felt warm under her bare feet, and she wanted nothing more than to stop, lie down on it, and never get up again. She paused at the doorway to their parents' bedroom. She'd always loved the smell of it—their mother's sweet lotions and their father's balmy colognes—but as she entered the room this time, she took quick, shallow breaths. She reached into the wardrobe for the whip: Mr. Koboko, as they called it when they were being playful. But there was nothing fun about the rough brown leather of the whip when it stung the skin, the three strands, like tentacles, curling around limbs and leaving welts wherever they touched. Ifechi felt light-headed at the thought of the koboko hitting her brother's flesh. Her hands shook as she presented the whip to her father, careful not to make contact with his skin.

"Go to your room," he said to Ifechi.

"No," their mother said. "Let her watch so she can learn."

So Ifechi watched as her brother lowered his pajama bottoms and gripped the edge of the dining table. Their father raised his hand with the koboko in it, and as he let it come down on Madu's buttocks, Ifechi squeezed her eyes shut. She heard the whoosh of the whip as it sliced the air, her father's grunts, her brother's gasps. After six lashes, Madu started to cry, letting go of the table to rub his behind. The next stroke of the whip landed on the back of Madu's hand, and he yelped. Tears stung Ifechi's eyes and she squeezed them even tighter. By the seventh stroke Madu was begging, his voice choked with phlegm: "Please Daddy Daddy please please I won't do it again!" Their father's response was a warning: "If you rub your buttocks again, I will start counting from one." That was when Ifechi stopped counting.

When it was finally over, Ifechi felt like her legs would crumple beneath her. Their mother's was the only dry face in the room: their father's was dripping with sweat. He let the koboko fall from his hand.

"What do you say?" their mother asked.

Ifechi looked from her to Madu as the seconds stretched into an eternity.

"What do you say?" she asked again, her tone sharp this time.

Madu stared at the ground. When he opened his mouth, his words were almost inaudible. "Thank you, Mummy. Thank you, Daddy."

They were sent to their room. With each shaky step Madu took, he grew taller in Ifechi's eyes—her big, strong brother who would protect her from the world. She promised herself she would never annoy him ever again, swore she would do anything he asked her to.

Madu fell onto his bed, burying his face in his arms. Ifechi could hear his sobs, hear their parents trying to argue quietly in the living room. She sat on the floor beside Madu's bed, rubbing his head and chanting, "Madu sorry, Madu sorry." Seeing that her brother was not comforted, Ifechi went to their dressing table and took the tub of Vaseline because, according to their mother, Vaseline could heal anything.

"Madu," she said, "should I rub Vaseline on your bum-bum?"

Ifechi got no response. When she started to tug on Madu's pajama bottoms, his arm shot out of nowhere, knocking the tub of Vaseline out of her hand and across the room, where it crashed into the wall.

· · ·

IT WAS TWO WEEKS LATER, and school had reopened after the long holidays. Before their mother got a job, she used to be around to take them to and from school. Now she only dropped them off in the mornings, with prayers and admonitions to guide them on their way back home: don't talk to strangers, look properly before crossing, never pick up any money or strange object from the ground, never *ever* ride on an okada to get home.

The first few times they'd walked home on their own, Madu had murmured his mother's warnings like a mantra, all the way from St. Gregory's College Road to Obalende roundabout. Gripping his sister's hand, he'd weaved through throngs of people at the bus stops. But those days now felt like a long time ago to Madu. He had grown accustomed to wading through the pulsating mass that was Obalende, with its countless yellow danfos and molues, conductors wooing passengers to faraway destinations across Lagos, men at the newspaper vendor's stand arguing about headlines they had no power to influence, traders luring passersby with wares from electronics to medicines to fake designer clothes imported from Aba.

As Madu and Ifechi turned onto their street, Madu released his sister's hand from his firm grip and slowed their pace. Ifechi hopped onto the rim of the gutter that ran beside the road. She spread her arms for balance as she walked, head bent to peer down into the gutter at the filmy green spirogyra that looked like alien vomit.

Madu pulled his sister off the gutter's rim and whispered to her, his breath brushing her ear. "One boy in my class, he brought a magazine to school that is like daddy's films. He showed me and some other boys during break."

"Haa, Madu," Ifechi said, covering her mouth with the palm of one hand. She stopped walking, forcing Madu to stop too.

Madu eyed his sister. "What? Why are you saying 'haa' like that?"

"Have you forgotten what happened with those films?" Madu resumed walking, and Ifechi followed. "Mummy said I should tell her if you do anything bad again."

Madu turned around to face his sister, and she noticed for the first time how much like their father he looked. She took a small step back.

"Good girl," Madu sneered. "So you want to report me to Mummy now, because I covered for you. Didn't you also join in watching the films? So you're now the good one, and Madu is bad."

"No," Ifechi muttered, looking at her feet.

"You're just a baby. You can run and tell Mummy if you want. That's what a baby would do." Madu leaned toward his sister, bringing his face as close to hers as possible without their skins touching. "Baaaabyyyy."

Madu stalked off and Ifechi stood watching him, tears filling her eyes. She blinked them away and ran to catch up with her brother.

. . .

IN BED THAT NIGHT, Madu heard their bedroom door creak open. He propped himself up on his elbows just in time to see Ifechi slip out through the doorway. The sound of the TV floated in from the living room, like something from a distant planet. And then all went quiet.

Many minutes passed before Madu got out of bed to follow after Ifechi. But then, as he opened the bedroom door, he heard the lash of the koboko, and Ifechi's cry right after. It slowly dawned on him what she'd done. It was foolish. *She* was foolish. Still, Madu couldn't help feeling a grudging admiration.

He was sitting up on his bed when Ifechi returned. He could see only her silhouette in the darkened room, but he knew her legs would feel like melting wax, pain burning through every nerve. He knew that the heat would spread from her behind, infecting the rest of her like a fever.

She fell facedown onto her bed, crying, her legs hanging out over the frame. Madu stood and went to the dresser. He felt around the top of it until his fingers touched the tub of Vaseline. He picked it up and took off the lid, then went to Ifechi and placed the tub on her bed, wrapping her slack fingers around it.

"Why did you tell them?" Madu asked.

As he watched his sister shudder, he felt a vague throbbing, like a phantom sensation, on the back of his hand where his father's whip had left a welt weeks ago. He reached for the Vaseline tub, scooped a dollop with his finger and began rubbing the spot in a circular motion.

It was a long time before Ifechi answered, her voice muffled by the pillow her face was buried in. "Because I am bad too."

Madu's stood still as he contemplated his sister's words, the sureness with which she had said them. He thought about the cassettes with their father's initials on them, all lined up in the cupboard like trigger bombs, waiting to explode and infect him and his sister with badness. He didn't know, now, what it meant to be good.

He went back to rubbing, his finger going around and around in an endless loop.

THE GIRL WHO LIED

THE FIRST TIME I SAW KEMI, SHE WAS CAUSING A SCENE. Everyone stopped to watch—the boardinghouse staff, the students they were checking in, and the parents carrying luggage into the hostels. In front of the hostels, in the large courtyard where cars were parked, a woman stood by the back door of a Land Cruiser with dark tinted windows, struggling to wrench herself free from Kemi, whose hands were locked around her middle. Kemi was holding on from behind, her face buried in the small of the woman's back. Dark sunglasses covered the woman's eyes, and she was muttering through stiff lips. The driver's door flew open and a short, harassed-looking man, who I guessed was the family chauffeur, hurried out of the car. He grabbed Kemi around the waist and pulled, his cheeks bulging. When he'd managed to separate Kemi from the woman, he carried her, kicking and screaming, in the direction of the school matron's house. I wasn't surprised by the laughter that had erupted around me, but I couldn't join in. Clearly, this girl was new here, like me. And she looked about eleven, so she would be a Junior Secondary 1 student, like me. I knew that if I were bolder, less inclined to shame, that could have been me, holding on to my mother's wrapper, begging her not to leave me at this school in the middle of nowhere.

. . .

THAT EVENING, after a short welcome address, the matron and other boardinghouse staff guided us J.S. 1 students, the new entrants, to our assigned rooms and beds. The rooms—each containing sixteen bunk beds and lockers—felt dense, the air inside thick with the heat of bodies. The windows were narrow, and the ceiling fans slow. I was shown to my bed and locker and immediately started unpacking my things, to distract myself from the homesickness that had already set in. For the thirteen weeks that the term lasted, there would be none of my father's catfish pepper soup on rainy nights, no more sitting in the cocoon of my mother's thighs as she massaged coconut oil into my scalp. I tried to take comfort in the chattering voices around me, but they were mostly from older students who were by now comfortable in this place that felt so strange to me. I glanced around and took count of the new students who'd been assigned to this room—they would be the wide-eyed ones in uniforms that were still crisp like mine, not frayed with time and usage.

I felt oddly pleased to find the girl from that afternoon sitting cross-legged on a lower bunk bed at the other end of the room, her body appearing smaller than it had before. She was chomping on something out of a red packet and staring into space. I stuffed the last of my things inside my locker and made my way to her bed, then stood there until she looked at me.

"My name is Tola," I said. When she didn't reply, I nodded at her boxes, massive and unopened on the floor. "Won't you unpack your things?"

She blinked up at me for a few seconds before looking away. "When I'm ready," she mumbled through the Maltesers in her mouth.

I waited for her to say more. When she didn't, I said, "You were the one holding your mummy's waist this afternoon. That was you."

She laughed. "You saw me, ehn? Was it good?"

I wasn't sure what she meant by "good," but I wanted her to know I could relate to how she was feeling. "I wish I could follow my parents back home too."

I was surprised when she sneered.

"What, you think I'm a baby?" she said. "Please, I was just playing."

Kemi resumed her staring and chewing, and I realized I'd been dismissed. As I went back to my locker, I decided that Kemi was spoiled—her mother's expensive car and her large boxes, surely filled with assorted goodies, the way she'd just spoken to me. I could never be friends with her.

I lay on the narrow bed after lights out, that first night at Badagry Model Secondary School, and stared into the dark. I imagined that, instead of standing by and watching my father's old Peugeot disappear after my parents had dropped me off, I'd chased the car out through the school gates and all the way back to our flat in Ajah. Traveling down to the school that afternoon, enduring the traffic at Mile 2 and Okokomaiko and, later, negotiating the potholed roads that ran through what looked like a vast coconut plantation, my mother had sung along with the radio while my father bobbed his head and tapped the steering wheel to the rhythm. Going back home with the car emptied of me, I wondered, could they have heard the songs the same way as before?

I liked to think not. I liked to think that my mother had cried, dabbing tears from her face and second-guessing bringing me here, and that my father had patted her shoulder with his free hand, comforting her in his quiet way. Here, I was by myself. It was dark, and as the room and its occupants slowly settled into sleep, I let go of the tears I had struggled to hold in all day.

· · ·

THE NEXT MORNING, I woke to Kemi shaking me.

"It's wake-up time," she said, peering into my face. She stood waiting, her towel wrapped around her, empty red bucket in hand, while I fumbled out of my nightdress. With the warm weight of sleep still snug around me, it felt natural to let her lead me, with my bucket, out of the room. The memory of her snobbery the day before had grown distant, replaced this morning by a wordless gratitude. Her towel, red to match her bucket and rubber flip-flops, seemed to glow before me, a beacon I felt compelled to follow. Outside, in the predawn dark, surrounded by other sleepy students, we lugged buckets of water from the taps to the communal bathroom, a square expanse of concrete floor enclosed by four walls and lit by fluorescent tubes. The light from the fluorescents attracted winged insects that buzzed around the bulbs before falling to the ground like confetti.

After surveying the bathroom with disdain, Kemi wove through the bathing girls. She led us to a vacant spot by a corner and set down her bucket. She unwrapped her body, folded her towel into a neat square, and set it to hang on the handle of her bucket as if she'd done this many times before. I tried not to stare at Kemi's chest, tried not to think how flat mine was in comparison. Instead, I set my gaze on Kemi's red bath bowl as it floated on the surface of the water in her bucket. From her bath bag, she took out a bar of soap that smelled sweet enough to eat and a fluffy pink sponge.

"Won't you remove your towel?" she asked me.

I kept a straight face and peeled my towel off, trying to mimic Kemi's ease. The warmth of my towel was replaced by a crippling self-consciousness as the air hit my naked skin. By the time I had my towel folded, Kemi had emptied two bowls of cold water over herself without making a sound and was lathering

soap onto her skin in vigorous strokes. I scooped up water in my
bath bowl and held it suspended, away from my chest.

"Is it cold?" I asked Kemi. It was an obvious stalling tactic,
and she stared at me until I looked away. I took a deep breath.
"Okay, I'll count to three and then pour," I announced to no
one in particular. "One . . . Two . . ."

Kemi's hand shot forward and she emptied a bowl of cold water
over my head. I shrieked, surprising myself and silencing the other
bathers for a moment with the sound. Kemi ignored my glare and
clapped her hands as she laughed, sending soapsuds flying.

When she was done laughing, she fixed me with a gaze so
solemn it was almost uncomfortable. "Don't worry," she said.
"I am here to help you." And then she smiled. "Even if it means
bathing you myself."

. . .

AROUND NOON THAT DAY, the J.S. 1 students were herded
into the school's assembly hall for the first item on our orientation program: the "School Tour." We were divided into small
groups. Kemi and I stuck together and, along with about fifteen
other students, ended up with a teacher who introduced himself
as Mr. Yusuf.

Mr. Yusuf led us from the assembly hall, where the tour
kicked off, to the dining hall, and then to the principal's house
and the school farm, which sat on the far end of the compound.
Then he steered us toward the hostels, giving a brief history
of each dorm. Next, we headed to an incongruous structure
that I'd glimpsed the day before, when my parents drove past
it on our way to the hostels. I'd been preoccupied with my
misery at the time, but now I could see that it was a cage. It
was about the width of four or five twin mattresses laid flat,

side by side, and was just high enough for an adult to stand in with their head grazing the corrugated aluminium roof. Half of the cage—the back wall and parts of the side walls—was made of concrete blocks roughly plastered with cement. The other half consisted of sheets of flat, crisscrossed metal bars. On the back wall of the cage, a large wooden box hung from a corner, furnished with a thin square of mattress foam and what looked like soiled strips of cloth. From inside this box, a large chimpanzee blinked at us. The chimpanzee's head jerked up as we neared the cage, and he watched us, still and alert. We stopped a respectful distance away and Mr. Yusuf pointed with his cane.

"This," he said, "is Chaka."

Chaka's muscled body was coated with dark brown hair, his eyes gold-flecked and somber. He pouted his lips and then spread them to show yellow teeth and dark gums. We chuckled as he picked his teeth with almost human fingers.

"Don't think that because Chaka sometimes acts like a person, you can play with him," Mr. Yusuf continued. "Remember that he is an animal, and he can be dangerous. You must never get too close to the cage."

"If he's dangerous, why is he here?" Kemi asked.

"Good question. But raise your hand when you want to say something," Mr. Yusuf said. He licked his lips. "Part of the land on which this great school was established . . . and when did I say the school was established?"

"Nineteen eighty-eight!" we all roared.

"Very good," Mr. Yusuf said with a proud grin. "But remember to raise your hands. Part of the land that was allocated for this school used to be a wildlife conservatory." His eyes darted from one face to another. "And who knows what a conservatory is?"

Nobody volunteered an answer. "Nobody?" he prodded.

Kemi sighed and, her voice heavy with reluctance, said, "A place where animals are kept."

"Brilliant! But like I said, raise your hand before you speak, ehn," Mr. Yusuf said. "A wildlife conservatory is a place for keeping and protecting wildlife, wild animals. So, part of the school, the area we now use as the farm, used to belong to a conservatory. When the government granted the land for the building of this great school, the animals were moved, but it seems Chaka was forgotten, or left behind. The authorities never came for him, so he has been here since, like an inheritance. Who knows what 'inheritance' means?"

Kemi rolled her eyes as eager hands shot up. The question got answered and the students were quiet again.

"Can we feed him?" somebody asked.

"No. Feeding Chaka is the job of Sovi, our head caretaker," Mr. Yusuf said. "You will see him around as time goes by. Never feed Chaka."

"Why can't we feed him?" Kemi asked, her hands fixed to her sides.

"I have just said that that is Sovi's job. You want to try feeding him so he can bite off your finger? That has happened before, to a stubborn student like you. After that incident, she got the nickname of Philo Four Fingers."

"Has Chaka ever killed anyone?" Kemi asked.

By now I wanted to clamp her mouth shut with my palm. Mr. Yusuf seemed to be struggling for words. Kemi filled the silence.

"What if he breaks this cage one day and escapes? What if he enters the hostels one night when everyone is sleeping?"

"Why are you asking these silly questions?" Mr. Yusuf said, glaring at Kemi.

"You said we could ask questions," Kemi answered, her face unflinching. I swore I heard a few students snickering, but I saw only straight faces when I looked around me.

Mr. Yusuf stared at Kemi a moment longer, then smoothed his mustache. "Moving on," he said as he started to march off.

The other students followed Mr. Yusuf quickly, me and Kemi falling behind.

After lights out that night, Kemi came to my bed. I had just started to drift off into sleep when she tapped my shoulder and whispered to me to move over. I blinked in the darkness, up at where I thought her face would be, and a question formed on my lips and lingered there. Without waiting for my response, she sat on my bed and pulled her legs up, forcing me to make room. I turned my back to her, but my eyes stayed open. She shifted around for a while, trying to find comfort. And she found it, molding her body into my stiff back. Her breath tickled my neck, and soon I could tell she was asleep. I stayed awake long after, not understanding my need to decipher the language her body spoke in sleep: one of murmurs, sighs, and grinding of teeth, unguarded and unrehearsed.

· · ·

IT WAS OUR FIRST SUNDAY at the school, and a visiting evangelist was part of the orientation program. At Badagry Model Secondary School, attendance at church or mosque was mandatory. Kemi said that because her family didn't go to church or mosque, she was free, here at school, to pick a side. I found this lack of definition in Kemi's life unsettling. In my family, church attendance was not subject to debate. Because my parents were both volunteer workers at our church—my father one of the Sunday school teachers and my mother a member of the choir—we would leave for church extra early after a quick liquid breakfast of hot Lipton tea, the promise of our usual Sunday lunch, my mother's rice and chicken stew, offering comfort through the duration of the hours-long service. There was none of my mother's food to return to here, but I managed to convince Kemi to come with me to the school chapel.

"All heads bowed, and all eyes closed." It was the evangelist. The silence was absolute.

"The Bible says," the evangelist thundered on, "that there will be weeping and gnashing of teeth! And it will be forever!"

I heard Kemi's frustrated groan beside me.

"You might think that you are still very young," the evangelist said, "but you are no longer children; you know right from wrong! God is watching, and all your sins will be played on a big screen in heaven on judgment day. All of you who tell lies, hell is waiting for you! You stole your bunkmate's bathwater? Hell is where you are headed! You lied to your parents for extra pocket money? Hell! Except! Except if you become born again today and turn from all those evil acts. Don't wait until tomorrow—what if you don't wake up in the morning? What if, as we are leaving here, the rapture happens and God calls His people home? Where will you go?"

The answer was silence, broken only by intermittent sniffles and coughs from around the hall.

"Who will come to Jesus today?" the evangelist said, his voice now gentle.

There was rustling and creaking of wood as students shifted on their benches. I cracked my eyes open long enough to glimpse anguished faces and raised hands, and to see that Kemi's fingers were tapping noiselessly on the bench. I closed my eyes again, raised my hand, and quietly repeated the words the evangelist said, inviting Jesus into my life yet again, just in case that first time with my parents three years ago hadn't been enough. In case my salvation had worn off.

I could breathe easier after the prayer; the air seemed lighter somehow. But the evangelist was not done. He raised his voice again.

"There is somebody here! You need special deliverance from the forces of darkness!"

"God, when will this end?" Kemi muttered.

"Yes! Somebody here, evil forces are oppressing you. They come to you in your dreams. Stand up and identify yourself and be set free!" he said.

The hall remained quiet for a while. Then, "It is me, Pastor!"

I opened my eyes to see Kemi already on her feet, her hands lifted high above her head. "It is me!"

Hushed exclamations filled the hall. Kemi's name was in the whispers.

"Today, you will be delivered. Come forward, sister!" the evangelist said, thrusting a fist up in the air.

As Kemi walked slowly to the front, I felt numb with dread. But I was also relieved that now, without having to ask, I had a possible explanation for Kemi's foray into my bed the other night. It must have been these people, these dreams the evangelist spoke of, that had scared her.

"Tell us what happened." The evangelist's voice was fatherly as he addressed Kemi. "The truth will set you free."

"I have been having . . . strange dreams," Kemi started. "This woman is always coming to me. She is very fair, with long hair, and she wears a long gown; a shiny gold gown. And a golden crown."

I thought there was a mythic quality to the woman that Kemi was describing—she sounded like a version of the storied ghost lady, Madam Koi Koi, haunting the dorms in her high-heeled shoes that went *koi koi* on the concrete floors.

"What does this woman do to you?" the evangelist prompted.

"She is always calling my name, saying"—and Kemi said this next bit in a voice I didn't recognize, a booming masculine voice—"'Kemi, Kemi, come and join the sisterhood! You have a mission!' Then I shout no and start running, and she starts chasing me . . . but . . . but when I turn back to look at her, her legs are not moving. And she doesn't even have any legs; she has a fish tail! And she's floating on air, and her long hair is made of snakes. Red snakes with tiny yellow eyes!"

"The devil is a liar," said the evangelist. "Sister Kemi, deliverance has come to you today. I will pray for you."

The service ended soon after, but the evangelist kept Kemi several minutes longer. I waited for her outside the chapel, and when she emerged I was surprised to see a smile on her face. It was not like any smile I had seen on the faces of the newly delivered. There was mischief in it. She gave me a quick wave and I waved back, expecting her to join me. Instead, she approached a group of girls standing in a huddle outside the hall. They had also attended the service, and as she got closer to them, their voices grew hushed. I watched Kemi talk with the girls, and before long they were howling with laughter. As though feeding on their mirth, Kemi grew more animated, her hands gesturing wildly. The girls doubled over, holding their sides and wiping their eyes. I found a place in the hall corridor and sat with my arms folded.

After the girls dispersed, Kemi came to me, the remnants of laughter on her lips. "I was telling them about the demon queen in my dreams."

"But you knew I was waiting for you," I said as I stood.

"You could have joined us," Kemi said. "I didn't ask you to sit here like a statue."

I ignored the sting of Kemi's words. "Why were they laughing? What was so funny?"

Kemi stared at me. "Don't tell me you believed it too," she said, her laughter coming sharp and unexpected now. "I should be in Hollywood!"

"You made the whole thing up? That's not funny, Kemi!"

"But it *is* funny," she sputtered. "You believed it, and those girls I was talking to just now, they believed it, until I told them I was acting. And the pastor! Did you see the pastor's face? I almost laughed right in front of him."

I marveled at Kemi's guts. I would never dare tell such an elaborate lie to a man of God. And those girls dying with laughter, they probably wouldn't either. Was this what happened when you weren't taught to believe in anything?

"You need to be careful, Kemi," I said. "What if something had happened to you?"

"Something like what?"

"Like with Ananias and Sapphira in the Bible!"

"Ana who? Abeg, nothing will happen. I was just joking around."

"You don't joke with God. I've heard of people who—"

"Relax, Tola!" Kemi said. "I don't know why you're so afraid of everything."

"I'm not afraid of everything!" I started to walk away, hoping that would settle it. Kemi followed.

"You're afraid of God," she said.

"The Bible says we should fear God."

"You're afraid of the matron and all the teachers."

"I *respect* them," I said, quickening my pace. "It's good home training."

"You're afraid of Chaka the chimpanzee."

"He bites people's fingers off!"

"You're even afraid of your classmates, J.S. 1 students like you!"

I stopped walking, causing Kemi to almost run into me. "That's not true!"

"Ehn? Then that day when Jemila tried to get in front of you in the queue at the dining hall, why didn't you say anything? You just let her, and I could see you didn't like it. If I hadn't yelled at her to go to the back of the line, she would have taken your place just like that. And you were just standing there, looking at her like a mumu. Are you a fool?"

I choked back my tears and opened my mouth to tell Kemi she was wrong. But my voice came out as a croak. I ran off to the library, where I hid my face in a book and cried, comforting myself with the thought that my parents would be proud of me for my handling of the situation, for the restraint I'd shown in keeping inside all the names I could have called her—with her big eyes and her forehead like a windshield. There I was, trying to look out for her, and she'd insulted me. She had no right to assume that she knew me so well after only a week. So I liked to avoid trouble; it didn't mean I was afraid of everything. And was it such a bad thing to let people take my place in a queue sometimes? It was better than starting a fight over it. I wondered why Kemi wanted to be my friend, since she thought I was such a fool. I decided that, from then on, I would keep my foolish self away from her and see how she fared. When she got into trouble, as was sure to happen the way she was going, it would not be my concern. I would watch and be secretly delighted every time she got punished. We'd see who turned out to be a fool.

When I heard the bell for dinner, I stayed put, ignoring my protesting stomach. Kemi might look for me in the dining hall, and I didn't want to talk to her ever again. I sat there in the library throughout night prep—Kemi would see me if I went to class—and for about an hour after, until there were only a few minutes before lights out. Inside our room, I had to pass by Kemi's bed to get to mine. She wasn't there, and it didn't matter. She was probably under the tree beside the hostel, reenacting her chapel performance for a fresh group of girls. I changed into my nightdress and lay on my bed, trying to take up more space than my skinny body needed. There would be no room for Kemi if she tried to squeeze in later. I closed my eyes.

When the first bell for lights out sounded, I felt a presence beside my bed.

"Tola."

I said nothing.

"Tola, I fetched your bathwater for you, for tomorrow."

I opened my eyes to see Kemi's hopeful face. She said, "There were many people at the taps. You should have seen how I struggled. See, I'm sweating." She wiped her forehead with the back of her hand and presented the evidence to me. "See."

I told myself I was accepting her unspoken apology so readily only because I'd been taught not to hold grudges. I resisted the urge to smile. "Thank you," I said.

She pushed my bucket of water under my bed for safekeeping. As she went back to her locker, I shifted on my mattress, to make space for her in case she needed it.

. . .

KEMI AND I WERE ON our way to the hostel one day after afternoon prep. The sun was beating down on us as Kemi told me yet another version of her appendicitis surgery story, how she'd woken up in the middle of the procedure and watched the doctors the rest of the way.

"I'm telling you, I saw when they took out my appendix," she said. "It was so red, but so tiny! And there was *so* much blood, as if somebody poured a whole bottle of Ribena on me. I mean the big-size bottle, not the small one."

As we passed by Chaka's cage, we recognized a few girls from our class standing around it, at a safe distance. They were making chimpanzee noises at Chaka, trying to get him to stop picking at his genitals and scare them off. Kemi stopped.

"You're all cowards!" she called out.

"Ha!" one of them replied. "You want to go near him? He'll bite you."

"What are you afraid of? He's just a chimpanzee," Kemi said.

"Oya, you go and touch it," someone else taunted. "Kemi the Brave."

"No, Kemi the Stupid." They all laughed.

"We'll see who's stupid," Kemi said, walking toward them. "I will go there, and I will touch that cage. Dare me."

"I dare you," one girl said. "In fact, I triple dare you!"

"Kemi . . . what are you doing?" I asked with a nervous chuckle.

Kemi shrugged off her backpack and headed toward the cage. The other girls stared, their skepticism giving way to awe with each step she took. I ran to catch up with Kemi and grabbed her arm.

"What are you doing?" I said. "Stop."

She tried to pull herself away but I held on, and soon we were locked in a bizarre tug-of-war. She turned around to face me, and with more force than I thought her capable of, she shoved me away from her. I watched from the ground, too stunned to move, as she resumed her march.

Chaka raised his head as Kemi approached the cage. Holding on to its metal bars, Kemi turned to look at me and the other girls, sticking out her tongue and shaking her bottom at us. The girls cheered Kemi on, and she danced harder for them, swinging her head from side to side. I kept my eyes on Chaka, so I saw when he made his move. But before my warning cry could register, he'd reached through the spaces between the bars of the cage and grabbed the front of Kemi's uniform. He held on, banging her body against the cage. The girls screamed as blood broke through the skin of Kemi's forehead and nose. They picked up stones and sticks to hurl at the chimpanzee, but the missiles just hit the metal of the cage with a clang and fell away. Just as I thought to run for help, Chaka let go of Kemi and she landed on the ground, buttocks first. Then she fell back, her body flat on the sand.

The other girls got to Kemi first, and they took hold of her arms and dragged her away from the cage. I ran to her.

"Kemi! Kemi, wake up!" I screamed, trying to shake her conscious. Tears were starting to blur my vision. A crowd was forming around us.

"Is she . . ." Whoever it was, they couldn't say the word that was on all our minds. I knelt there staring down at Kemi's still body. I should have tried harder to stop her. I should have stood in her way, fought her to the ground.

Kemi's eyes popped open and her swollen lips spread wide. I found the white of her smile, the ease of it, disturbing, at odds with the blood on her face. She sprang into a sitting position, her head almost colliding with mine. The girls broke into a cheer. They helped Kemi to her feet, brushing sand from her clothes and hair. Like a small wave, the crowd carried her a few feet away, leaving me kneeling, watching the imprint her body had left in the sand. I retrieved Kemi's backpack with a shaky hand. Chaka had settled into his box bed, and Kemi, cocooned within her newest crowd, acted out being banged against Chaka's cage, her body convulsing back and forth. Somebody offered her a tissue, and she held it against her forehead. I took Kemi by her free hand.

"Let's go to the sick bay."

She wrested her hand from mine. "For what?"

I couldn't keep the frustration from my voice. "Kemi, there's blood on your face."

She waved the bloodied tissue at me. "I have this."

She walked toward the hostel, her mesmerized crowd following, growing, as more girls came to hear of her latest feat. I didn't know how to sort through the feelings roiling inside me: anger at Kemi for her recklessness, resentment at being cast aside yet again for an excited audience. There was also fear. And with it, confusion. Because in that moment I was afraid both of her—and what she might do next—and for her. I forced myself to focus on the wounds that I and everyone else could see, the cuts on her face. I couldn't physically drag Kemi to the sick bay, so I considered going there myself and telling the nurse of her injuries. If the nurse sent for Kemi, Kemi would be forced to go. But she would never forgive me for going behind her back like that. Plus, reporting the incident to the nurse could result in the matron getting involved, and Kemi had already been summoned twice by the matron for talking back to the senior prefect. A third offense would go on her record.

I looked for Kemi in the swelling crowd. I couldn't see her anymore, but I knew she was there, swallowed up by her many followers. Her backpack remained in my hand, weighing me down.

· · ·

I KNEW SHE WOULD COME to my bed that night. I heard her approaching, and I turned my back and feigned sleep, resisting the tension that crept into every muscle. She got onto my bed.

Her face felt wet tucked into the space between my shoulder blades, and it occurred to me that she might be crying. Even as I resolved not to yield to her, I felt my anger from that afternoon melting away. I wanted to say something to comfort her, but I lay still instead, let her body curve into mine.

. . .

MY MOTHER CAME ON THE afternoon of the first visiting day of the term, as she'd promised. The courtyard in front of the hostels was crowded with cars and the families of students, just as it had been the day I'd arrived. I had been standing on the veranda outside the hostels since lunchtime, waiting for my mother, craning my neck to look up the road, and hoping Kemi would get bored and go inside without me. But she was still standing beside me when I made out a figure with my mother's rolling walk.

As my mother approached, it struck me how tired she looked. I welcomed the familiar pattern on her Ankara blouse and wrapper, but I could see now how badly the colors had faded. I pictured Kemi's mother, her face smooth like a mannequin's, her thighs sheathed in denim trousers that my mother could never pull off. And there was that big shiny car Kemi's mother had. For the first time, it bothered me that all my family had was the squeaky Peugeot, and I was glad my mother hadn't come in it.

My mother spotted me and called out with a wave and a smile, and when I went running to her, Kemi followed. I stepped into my mother's open arms and buried my face in her chest—her clothes smelled like smoke and stew spices—my happiness mingling with mild unease at seeing my mother through Kemi's eyes. When I let go, my mother handed me the Bagco bag she'd brought with her. I thanked her and bit back my disappointment at how light it felt. My mother looked me over, complaining about the mosquito bites that marked my arms and how I'd lost weight. She eventually noticed Kemi hovering beside us with a half smile.

"Is this your friend?" my mother asked.

"Yes, Ma," Kemi answered for me with a cute curtsy. "My name is Kemi."

My mother smiled and spread her arms at Kemi, who accepted the hug with a small, delighted laugh. As my mother let Kemi go, she noticed the fading bruises and scabs on her forehead, remnants from her encounter with Chaka. "What happened to your face?"

"It's nothing, Ma," Kemi said. "I got up one night to pee and it was dark, so I didn't see the door. I walked into it."

My mother frowned her concern as she examined Kemi's face, clicking her tongue, trailing her fingers around the bruises, asking if they still hurt. Kemi said no, and as my mother fussed some more, Kemi's eyes found mine. I could almost hear her daring me to tell the truth about her face. I looked away.

At my mother's suggestion we walked to one of the school shops to get drinks. As we went, she explained that my father was out of town for work and that he sent his love. She talked about home, how it was so quiet without me there and how she had put off hiring an assistant at her hair salon for yet another month. As she spoke, she would turn to Kemi every so often, as if to make sure she was still there, and ask how she was. We sat down at the shop with our drinks, and Kemi stayed the whole time, making my mother laugh with embellished stories of our first days at the school, like how she'd had to chase me around the large bathroom with a bowl of water on our first morning to get me to take my first cold bath. I watched Kemi charm my mother, part of me thinking I should be upset, or at least a little jealous. But there was a need in Kemi that seemed new to me, and not for the first time, I felt something like pity for my friend.

Kemi remained with us until my mother was ready to leave. When it was time, I took the bag my mother had brought inside the hostel, to empty it into my locker, and then I went back out to walk with her to the school gates. My mother told Kemi that she didn't have to come with us, but Kemi insisted. Kemi was quiet as we walked, and remained so when we reached the gates. My mother held both our hands and prayed for us and, before turning to leave, took me aside.

"Your friend, she seems a little sad. Is she okay?"

I glanced at Kemi, who for some reason was intently examining the sandy ground. "Yes," I said.

"Are her parents coming to visit?"

"She told me her mother's coming."

"Okay," my mother said, a shadow of a frown on her face. Because I recognized something in my mother's expression, a mild concern, I wanted to reassure her, and perhaps myself as well, that Kemi was indeed all right.

"Hmm, Mummy, Kemi's family ehn, they're very rich." I heard the hint of pride in my own voice, like I had contributed to this wealth somehow. "You should see the car they used to bring her to school. And all the provisions she came with, three full boxes. Very rich, Mummy. She said they go to London and America for holidays every year."

"Oh, you see," my mother said. "I was right about this school. If a family like that chooses to send their child here, then this is a good school."

"Ehn . . . but the dining hall food here is not like home food. And we wake up at five every morning, except Saturdays and Sundays. And the teachers like to cane us—"

"Tolani, stop complaining," my mother scolded gently. "You should be thankful that you can come to school here. You know how much we are paying."

"Yes, Mummy," I mumbled at the ground.

"Don't worry, before you know it six years will pass and you'll finish from here," she said. "What am I even saying, by the time you become a senior you won't remember all of your whining. You'll want to stay another six years!"

"No, Mummy," I laughed. "Never, never, never."

She looked at Kemi, who was now squatting and drawing figures in the sand with a twig.

"I'm glad you've made a friend. I hope you two will be positive influences on each other. Remember what the Bible says about friends: evil communications . . ."

"Corrupt good manners," I said.

Was Kemi corrupting my "good manners"? I didn't think so. I still prayed every night like my parents had taught me to, and before every meal. I still studied hard and didn't cheat, and I tried to be kind to people.

Looking at my mother's face, I wanted to tell her all about Kemi. About her sleeping in my bed some nights. About how she made up stories, like that day in church; how she mocked teachers behind their backs, and how I had to constantly see to it that she didn't get into too much trouble. I wanted to tell her that Kemi liked to hike up the skirt of her uniform when she sat in class, or anywhere, and that she kept doing it even after Mr. Alabi had caned her six times, even when she knew people could see her underwear. I wanted to tell her that Kemi liked the sight of her own blood, that she cut her nails so close to the skin that spots of red sprouted, and that she no longer bothered to pretend it was a mistake. I wanted to tell her about Chaka and how, even after that incident, Kemi still sometimes walked dangerously close to his cage, cackling when I rushed to pull her away. But I wasn't sure my mother would see that, in spite of all these things, Kemi was not "evil."

After giving me and Kemi final hugs, my mother left. I watched her through the school gates until she got onto a bus, and then Kemi and I walked back to the hostel in silence. In the weeks since I'd been at the school, I'd started to get used to it: the wake-up bell at 5:00 AM, cold showers, the dining hall meals with runny stews and pieces of meat the size of Maggi cubes. But now that I'd seen my mother again, the homesickness returned. I missed my mother's little salon and the smell of Ultra Sheen, her spicy efo riro with shaki and kpomo. I tried not to cry, but I couldn't help it. I felt ashamed of my tears, the snot dripping from my nose, and hoped Kemi would pretend not to notice. She didn't. She said my face swelled like a pumpkin when I cried, and she went on to retell the story of the last Halloween she had spent with her cousins in America and how the carved pumpkin had appeared in her dream that night to take her on an adventure. I let Kemi's voice wash over me, grateful to her for sparing me, in her own way.

· · ·

IT WAS 6:00 PM WHEN Kemi got a message saying she had a visitor. She sprang from her bed, tugging at my arm and saying I had to meet her mother now. We hurried out of the hostel and saw the only car left outside: the black Land Cruiser, looking bronzed in the light of the setting sun. As we approached the car, the driver's door opened and I recognized the chauffeur from the first day. He flashed uneven teeth at us.

"Ah, Kemi," he said. "How are you?"

Kemi looked past him, into the back of the car. "Where's my mum?"

"Em, she traveled to Dubai today," he said quietly, as though he was afraid to be heard. "I just dropped her at the airport; that's why I'm late. But she sent plenty of things for you—"

Kemi ran back into the hostel, leaving me with the driver. After a moment of awkward silence, he went behind the car to open the boot. He hefted out two large bags.

"Please . . . take these bags to her, ehn. They're from her mother."

I took the bags by the handles and watched him drive away. Inside, I set the bags down in front of Kemi's locker. As on that first day, she was sitting on her bed, staring at nothing. I sat beside her.

"Sorry your mum couldn't come," I said. And, after a while, "Won't you look at what she sent for you?"

"You look."

I opened the bag and found enough in it to last a whole term: bright, colorful boxes of cereal—the imported kind that my mother always skipped at the supermarket in favor of plain Nasco cornflakes—a pack of sugar cubes, tins of milk, cans of sardines, a large bag of Ijebu garri, groundnuts, chocolate chip cookies, juices, and sodas. My bag had contained a sack of garri, a packet of sugar, one small bottle of groundnuts, one tin of Milo, and one sachet of powdered milk. I opened Kemi's locker and started to arrange the provisions in it, cheered by the thought that as her friend I would get to partake of them. Then I glanced at Kemi's face and immediately felt guilty. It was a good thing I'd let her have my mother for the afternoon.

. . .

THAT NIGHT, AFTER LIGHTS OUT, the J.S. 1 students in my room gathered around Kemi's bed, as we sometimes did. Kemi sat in the middle of her bed, and the rest of us spread out around her on the bed and floor, waiting for one of her stories. The mood was festive, resonant with the students' joy at seeing their families. The dorm prefects were not enforcing the rules of lights out, too busy breaking said rules with their own friends. We passed around a bowl of home-cooked fried rice, the glow of a flashlight the only illumination.

"Kay-Kay," one of the girls said. They called her Kay-Kay, these people who were not her friends. "Is it true you've seen Madam Koi Koi?"

School lore had it that Badagry Model Secondary was built on the grounds of an old cemetery. According to the origin story, Madam Koi Koi was a teacher in the early days of the school. She'd had an affair with a former principal, and had ended up murdered, poisoned by the principal's jealous wife. Her body was buried in the conveniently located cemetery, the truth covered up, and now she roamed the school grounds seeking a female body to possess so she could go in search of her lover. I doubt that any of us believed she was real, but there seemed to be an unspoken contest to come up with the most terrifying stories of the ghost lady sightings. Kemi had told her own Madam Koi Koi story many times.

"Ugh, we've heard that story," somebody groaned.

"Yes, something new!"

I wished I could make them disappear, these girls who kept pecking at her, looking to be entertained. Some had even taken to calling her KKTV, and she welcomed it, switching accents as she spoke and making her voice scary and then soft, acting out her tales with flair and contorting her face into masks as she held her flashlight under her chin in the dark. But watching her in those moments, I imagined a puppy performing tricks for its owner for a treat. Kemi didn't just want their attention, she seemed to need it, like it was the only thing keeping her from falling into a dark hole. Did nobody else see this? Or was I just making things up to prove to myself that she needed me? To convince myself that those nights when she came to my bed, when I sacrificed sleep and matched my breathing with hers and made my body into shapes that allowed her to be, I was somehow saving her?

"Have I told you about my appendicitis operation?" Kemi said. There was a chorus of yeses. Kemi continued, "And how I traveled to London with my mummy and saw the queen?"

Kemi ran through a list of stories, all familiar, all recycled times over. Then she fell silent.

"KKTV has closed," somebody said, with a sigh that was really a challenge. "Turn off the TV."

These girls, they came and went from Kemi's life as they pleased, taking the bits of her that they enjoyed, leaving the rest for me.

"Have I told you," Kemi said finally, her voice a whisper, "about the Man of Night?"

She paused, and we grew still with her. The murmuring of the other students in the room faded into silence in my ears.

"He lives in the shadows," Kemi continued. "And . . . you know how in horror films, something will happen in a dream, but the person feels it when they wake up? That's what the Man of Night feels like. He will come when you're sleeping. He will whisper things in your ear. You can't see him. Even if you open your eyes, all you'll see is black. But you can feel his hands . . . touching you. But nobody will believe you when you tell. 'You've come again with your stories,' that's what they'll say. Because you're the only one who knows. You're the only one he comes to at night."

After a long silence, one listener asked, "So what happens next?"

"He follows you," Kemi said. "He follows you everywhere."

"Is he here now?"

The girls looked around with exaggerated trepidation, waiting for Kemi to raise the tension, say something to make them shudder in fearful delight. But Kemi stayed quiet, ignoring the girls' questions and promptings. This story, without scary voices or song and dance, was not the kind they had come to expect from their beloved KKTV. I, too, was struck by this Man of Night, but in a different way than the other girls. Something about him felt real. Perhaps because Kemi did not perform him like she did her other stories, perhaps because of the way she let her stillness be the story. Perhaps because, as the girls peeled themselves away, Kemi allowed herself to sit there with nothing more to give, nothing left to make them stay.

· · ·

THE SKY WAS CLOUDLESS the next afternoon, perfect for laundry day. Inside the dorm, I stood beside Kemi's bed, my dirty clothes and a sachet of detergent stuffed in my bucket, trying to get her to come out with me.

"I don't feel well," she said, her face buried in her pillow. I was skeptical. Any moment now, she could be entertaining a small crowd, as though a switch somewhere inside her had been flipped. I was not doing her laundry.

"Sorry, ehn," I said in my sweetest voice. "I'm going to wash by the well behind the hostel. You can meet me there when you're feeling better."

There were three other girls washing their clothes under the tree near the well when I got there. I found a spot under the tree and heaped my dirty laundry on the ground, and then I lowered a rubber fetching pail into the light brown water in the well and filled my bucket.

I was rinsing out my clothes when I saw Kemi approaching in the distance. I noticed she wasn't carrying any clothes, and I looked back down at my washing. I knew that if I looked at her sulking face long enough, it would persuade me to do her washing yet again. When she got to me, I would try my best to avoid that face.

I heard the screams first, and then there was a splash. I looked up to see the other girls rush toward the well, and I followed, fighting to disbelieve what I suspected had happened. My fingers felt wooden as I clutched the rim of the well and leaned over to look inside it. Kemi was there at the bottom of the well, the water reaching to her chest, looking up at us. There was a patch of red on her right cheek where her skin must have scraped against the side. Other than that, she seemed unharmed. I did not let myself imagine what might have happened had the well been deeper, with enough water to bury her completely. One of the girls ran off to get help as more students, alerted by the screams, surrounded the well.

"Kemi! Are you okay?" I called down. "What happened? How did you fall inside?"

Another girl, one of the three who had been by the well earlier, glanced at me. "She didn't fall," she said. "She jumped."

It shouldn't have made sense to me that Kemi would jump into a well, but it did. The well had a high concrete rim; it would be difficult for anyone to fall in by accident. And there was that whole thing with Chaka, and the feeling it had left me with: a sense of the inevitable. I had never pictured Kemi at the bottom of a well, staring up at the world, but seeing her now, I got the feeling that this, or some version of it, was always going to happen.

"Move away . . . make way," the matron panted, running toward us. I saw some of the tension on her face ease when she looked inside the well and saw that Kemi was conscious. She grabbed the closest girl she could reach.

"Go and call Sovi immediately!" she said. "Tell him to bring his strong rope."

The matron shouted questions down at Kemi as we waited for the caretaker. But Kemi remained silent and wouldn't look at anyone. Sovi appeared shortly with a length of rope coiled around one shoulder. His walk was not any brisker than usual, and he had on the same brown shorts and white singlet he always wore. The matron pointed at the well, and Sovi bent to take a look. His face, when he straightened up, registered no surprise at finding a girl inside the well. He considered his surroundings and then walked to the tree where I and the other girls had been washing our clothes. He took the rope from his shoulder and tied one end around the tree's trunk, tugging at it to test its hold. Satisfied, he uncoiled the rope all the way to the well and lowered the other end down into it. Sovi gripped the rim of the well and eased himself over slowly, one leg finding a foothold first, and the other joining in. Then he transferred his grip from the well's rim to the rope. His muscles bunched and strained as he made the slow journey down the well.

When Sovi emerged from the well, the matron peeled Kemi from his back. I fought my way through the students to Sovi's side, where Kemi was laid down on the ground, her right leg jutting at an odd angle. Her clothes were dripping wet, and tears escaped from her eyes, which were squeezed shut against the pain. I tried to comfort her with words I no longer remember, but if she heard me, she gave no sign. At the matron's direction, Sovi lifted Kemi off the ground. They started toward the sick bay, and I followed, leaving the gawking students behind.

At the sick bay, Sovi put Kemi down on a bed while the matron talked with the nurse. Kemi kept her eyes closed, and I knelt beside the bed and stroked her hair, watching the wetness from her clothes spread through the bedsheets. The nurse briefly examined Kemi's leg and shook her head; she needed a proper hospital. Kemi was scooped up into Sovi's arms again, and the matron, the nurse, Sovi, and I hurried toward the matron's house. There, Sovi gently laid Kemi across the back seat of the matron's car, and the matron drove toward the school gates.

. . .

TWO DAYS LATER, we the four witnesses stood in single file before the principal, the matron, and Kemi's mother.

"You girls were there when it happened?" the principal asked from behind her wide desk, looking at each of us in turn.

"Yes, Ma," we answered.

Kemi's mother sat on the other side of the principal's desk, her back turned to the principal as she stared at us. Her face gave nothing away, and her eyes reminded me of the tinted, polished windows of her car. The matron stood beside the principal like a sentry.

"Please, Ma," I asked, not directing my words at any particular adult, "where is Kemi?"

"She's in the hospital," the principal said, looking slightly displeased. "She broke her leg, but other than that she's fine. Now, tell us what happened. Kemi has refused to talk."

The other girls looked everywhere but at the panel of adults.

"Did she fall into the well by accident?" the matron prompted. "Did someone push her?"

"There is nothing to be afraid of," the principal said, impatience creeping into the soothing tone she was trying to adopt. "Nobody is going to punish you for anything you say here."

"She fell, Ma," one of the girls said.

"It's true, Ma," the others agreed quickly. One added, "She was bending, to draw water, then she fell inside the well. That's all we saw."

I was not surprised that they would lie. We all knew that saying Kemi had jumped could get her into trouble. The principal and matron looked relieved. Kemi's mother's face stayed blank.

"Well," the principal sighed, "the doctor said she'll be fine once her leg heals. We thank God for that."

"Good thing that well is not very deep," the matron said. "Or we might be telling a different story now—"

"She jumped," I said. I felt everyone in the room turn to me, but I kept my focus on the wall behind the principal's head.

"You said what?" the principal asked.

"Kemi jumped," I said. "Nobody pushed her, and she didn't fall in by accident. She wasn't trying to fetch water; she didn't even have a bucket with her. She just came, and she . . . she jumped."

Kemi's mother leaned forward and glared at me. "You're lying," she said. Her voice was raspy, like she was recovering from a cold. "Why would she jump into a well?"

I didn't look away. "I don't know why."

My heart was pounding in my chest, and I wanted to run from that room, from all those people staring at me, from Kemi's mother and her face like porcelain. But I stayed put. If I could make her believe me, maybe she would look deeper, see beneath Kemi's surface, beneath the bravado and theatrics, see what I had sensed but could not put into words.

"Has she been showing signs of sadness or depression?" the principal asked.

The other girls were quick to shake their heads. One of them even chuckled, like Kemi and sadness being mentioned in the same sentence was absurd.

"Kemi ke?" the matron said. "Everybody knows her, she's a very lively girl."

"Lively" was one way to put it. But why wasn't the matron also saying that Kemi had difficulty following rules, or that she'd had cause to summon Kemi twice already in the six weeks the term had lasted?

The principal turned to Kemi's mother. "Madam, has Kemi ever showed any . . . troubling signs at home?"

"Nothing troubling, per se." She gave an elegant shrug. "She has an active imagination, but we're all used to it."

"Thank you, girls," the principal said after a long silence. "You can go."

The other girls filed out, trying to make as little sound as possible. I didn't move. I wanted to say more, but I didn't know what exactly. I opened my mouth, swallowed air.

The principal looked at me. "You too."

Outside the office, I paused just beside the door, left it ajar. I heard the matron say that I couldn't be sure of what I'd said, that eleven-year-olds weren't in the habit of throwing themselves into wells. Then someone shut the door from the inside.

As I approached the hostel later that afternoon, after prep, I saw Kemi's mother's car. It was empty. I wondered if she was still in the principal's office and, if so, what they were talking about. I thought about finding the driver and giving him a message to take to Kemi, that I was thinking of her. Kemi's mother suddenly emerged from the hostel, rolling one of Kemi's wheeled boxes on the ground. Behind her, the driver carried Kemi's mattress in a bundle on his head, a bag of her things in his other hand. Our eyes met and he looked away.

. . .

I HAVE ASKED MYSELF, in the twelve years that have passed since I last saw her, would I still have told the truth that day if I'd known it would mean never seeing Kemi again? I would like to say yes, that eleven-year-old me was capable of putting Kemi's needs before mine, that I would have suffered the loss anyway if it meant a chance at saving her. But a part of me doubts this. Maybe I would have preferred a broken Kemi over no Kemi, and ignored all the things I didn't understand. Maybe I'd have convinced myself that I could protect her and love her into wellness with time, all by myself.

After it was clear Kemi wasn't coming back to Badagry Model Secondary, I wrote her a letter, and only afterward did I realize I had no address to send it to—all I knew was that she lived in Ikoyi. Even now, over a decade later, I still type *Kemi Oyewole-Kamson* into a Google search every once in a while. I find many Kamsons, even a few Kemi Kamsons, but I don't find her. Unlike many former students from that school who've shown up in my People You May Know tab on Facebook, Kemi remains elusive.

Some days, Kemi is so real to me that I can feel her breath on my back, hear her ringing laughter. Other days, she's just a ghost haunting the halls of my mind.

BURNING

ADANNA KNOWS HER MOTHER'S FACES. THERE IS A FACE for the days when she wakes up with a light in her eyes and they stay home eating too-sweet balls of puff-puff, batches and batches pouring out of her mother's pan and forming small steaming hills on every surface in the kitchen. On days like this, they rewatch her mother's collection of Nollywood films, in which good and evil are separate like oil and water, and justice comes swift from heaven in the form of lightning. On other happy days, they visit Tejuosho Market and make their way through a maze of clothes shops, male traders whistling at their backsides and grabbing at their arms, and Adanna's mother throwing smiles at them over her shoulder while Adanna tries to shrink herself to nothing. When they return home with piles of clothes, Adanna's mother says with a conspiratorial wink, "Good thing it's your grandfather's money paying for all this."

There come the days when her mother is unable to drag herself out of bed. On these days, her face is pale with fear, her eyes darting at the slightest sound. Adanna's mother buries this face in a pillow and refuses to get up, and Adanna makes her own breakfast, a cup of Milo and two slices of bread, and eats it standing in the quiet kitchenette. Then, in the bedroom she and her mother share, she puts on her blue shirt and pink pinafore and heads for the front door, hoping to hear her mother's voice call out at the last moment with an offering, to walk with her maybe, or a promise to be there when the bell rings at the end of the school day. One time, her mother did call out to her from under the bedding, told Adanna to hold on as she put on a T-shirt and tied a wrapper around her waist. She took Adanna's hand along with a deep breath, and they walked out the door together. The pressure of her mother's grip, the quiet slapping of her slippers against her feet, made up for those mornings Adanna had walked alone. With her mother holding her hand, Adanna would not have to tug at strangers' sleeves at the busy junction and ask for help to cross the road. But barely halfway to school, her mother's fingers went limp and let go of Adanna's. Her mother sank, squatting in the street and burying her face in her hands. Adanna stood stunned, feeling naked as strangers stared at them. She wanted to keep walking and ignore the anchor pulling her down, pretend that the moaning ball of flesh had no connection to her. She resisted the urge to scream at her mother, at the sky, at all the people watching them but moving on, minding their business. Instead, she knelt on the warm asphalt and rubbed her mother's back in circles, around and around. The noise of traffic and hawkers and conversation faded until all she could hear was her mother's muffled sobbing. When Adanna's mother stood again, it was Adanna's hand holding hers, guiding her back home.

There are days when her mother wears her heavy face, the skin around her mouth dragged down by the weight of things Adanna cannot know. On these days, her mother sits in their shared bed and cries endless streams of tears, pushing aside Adanna's attempts at comfort—an embrace, a glass of water, a wad of tissues—until Adanna learns to keep her distance. She sequesters herself in a corner of the room and imagines the tears as a flood that rises and rises until their bodies, hers and her mother's, become two islands separated by infinite seas. Sometimes the tears are accompanied by mournful Igbo songs that sound at once ominous and beautiful.

Some days, her mother wakes with a face as hard as stone. On a day like this, nearly a year ago, Adanna and her mother ended up at the top of a prayer mountain in a sleepy Osun town, feet bleeding from their barefoot climb, kneeling before a wailing prophetess who made a show of expelling unnamed devils from Adanna with a wrought-iron crucifix. It is also on a day like this that Adanna finds herself enduring the scrutiny of a cross-eyed dibia dressed in all white.

. . .

ADANNA ADJUSTS IN HER SEAT, shifting her weight slowly so her movements go unnoticed. From the corner of her eye, she can make out her mother's dark figure. She does not dare turn her head to look, doesn't even dare to blink. She forces her gaze to stay on the white space high up on the wall. She has selected this spot carefully. If she keeps looking at it, she won't see the dibia seated on the floor before her, a white circle painted in chalk around his roving eye. She will not see the red cloth hanging on the wall behind him, adorned with cowries and the skulls of small animals. She will not see the clay pot in the corner, its rim bearing sinister testimony—bird feathers, drops of blood. Adanna's tongue prods the soft flesh on the inside of her cheeks; she remembers the faint coppery taste of past self-inflicted wounds.

"This is she?"

The dibia's voice is the sound of dead palm fronds rubbing together. Adanna looks into the chalk-rimmed eye before she can catch herself. The eyeball jerks about, restless in its confines.

Adanna's mother answers yes.

In her ten years on earth, Adanna has learned a few things, like be patient, be ready for anything, because you never know which Mummy will wake up beside you on any given morning. On the bus ride over—Adanna's mother carrying her on her lap to avoid paying two fares—questions burned in Adanna's mind. But even with the intimacy of skin on skin, her buttocks rubbing against her mother's thighs with every sway and jerk of the bus, Adanna knew to ask nothing.

When they arrived at this place, it took a while for Adanna to realize they were at a dibia's. She'd never seen a real-life dibia, and all the ones she had seen in movies operated out of thatch structures set in forests in the middle of nowhere. From there, they consulted with gods and spirits, and dispensed medicines and charms wrapped in leaves. She would never have imagined that a green duplex on a quiet street in Gbagada, three doors down from a Montessori school, could house a dibia.

The dibia says something in Igbo. Adanna's mother digs into her handbag and places a wad of naira notes, held together by a rubber band, before him. The money disappears into the folds of his robe. They carry on their conversation, casting occasional glances at Adanna that confirm, though she does not understand Igbo, that she is indeed the topic of interest.

When Adanna's mother and the dibia stand, Adanna rises too.

"Stay here," the dibia says to Adanna, before guiding her mother into the darkness hidden behind a white curtain.

The silence swallows Adanna. She looks at the square of red cloth, chooses an animal skull to focus on. She stares so hard that she imagines the skull rebuking her for being rude. She closes her eyes and tries to catch snatches of her mother's voice, but there is no sound. Adanna tucks a sliver of skin from inside her cheek between her teeth and bites down.

When Adanna opens her eyes again, the dibia is back in his place on the mat. Her mother is beside her.

"I will ask you some questions," the dibia says. "Answer quick quick. Don't think, don't lie. I will know if you lie."

Adanna turns to her mother.

"Look at him," her mother says, and she obeys.

The dibia hurls a question at Adanna. "You are ogbanje, are you not?"

Adanna's head swivels back to her mother, to confirm that the question is real, that the dibia truly is asking if she is like one of those spirit children in scary movies who play in groups at night, their bodies covered in white, delighting in the cries of their desperate mothers begging them to stay in the world of humans and not die for the umpteenth time. Adanna knows from the movies that a woman cursed with an ogbanje is locked in a cycle, birthing the same child in different bodies, a child destined to die and be reborn, and die and be reborn, and die . . .

"Answer the question," Adanna's mother says through gritted teeth.

"You are ogbanje," the dibia says.

"I—no!"

"You know ehn?" the dibia says. He exchanges a look with Adanna's mother, as if to say, *Did I not tell you?*

Adanna opens her mouth to protest, but the image of the prophetess from the prayer mountain steals the words from her lips. A whirlwind in a red robe, the prophetess had waved her crucifix at the sky and screamed, "Devil, be gone!" at Adanna for hours. Then she'd taken all of their money as payment for the spirits so the exorcism would be permanent, forcing Adanna and her mother to beg for rides back to Lagos. At the time, Adanna had looked upon the prophetess as a bad actor. But now, with the dibia staring her down, Adanna wonders if the prophetess truly had seen something evil in her, if her being an ogbanje is the explanation for all the things in her life that feel broken. Like her father dropping dead a week after she was born, his heart refusing to beat on. Like her mother and her changing faces.

"If you say you are not ogbanje, then answer my questions," the dibia says.

"Answer his questions, Ada," her mother echoes.

"How many spirit friends do you have?" the dibia asks. "Do you see your spirit friends when you dream? What do you talk about with them? Do you eat in your dreams? How many spirit husbands do you have? Do you dream of dying? When have you planned to die?"

The questions continue, so quickly that Adanna can barely separate one from the next, cannot find a space to insert her voice. Even if she could, her answers would change nothing. Unlike the prophetess, and all the ones before, the dibia has given a name to her badness. And this name, ogbanje, is one her mother will hold on to.

Her heart is pounding now, and the dibia's words meld into a cacophony of sound that becomes a ringing in her ears. She reaches to touch her mother's thigh, but her hand is slapped away. She wonders if her mother will leave her here, make her sleep in this room with the skulls and the white walls and the dibia's chalked eye watching her all night, unblinking, from behind the curtain. The ringing gets louder, and when Adanna cannot take it any longer, she places her palms over her ears and recites the thirty-six states and capitals of Nigeria in her head, in alphabetical order, to drown out the noise.

The room is quiet when Adanna reaches Zamfara state. Her mother is still there beside her, and Adanna feels grateful enough to cry.

The dibia clears his throat. "Madam," he says to Adanna's mother, his unchalked eye never leaving Adanna, "in three days, you will bring her back here. She will tell us where she buried her iyi-uwa."

. . .

IN THE DAYS BEFORE the next visit to the dibia, Adanna does not go to school. Each morning, her mother says from beneath her pillow, "No school today." But then, instead of staying buried under her wrapper, her mother drags herself into the kitchen to make Adanna's favorite meals: fried eggs with plantains so ripe the slices stick together, moin-moin with smoked fish, jollof rice. She hovers nearby to watch Adanna eat, her face taut with expectation.

Adanna knows what her mother wants. The word beats like a pulse in the back of her mind. *Iyi-uwa.* An object? A person? A spirit? She asks her mother what it is, this iyi-uwa. The answer is silence and a reproving stare, as though Adanna has just asked her mother what her own name is.

Adanna plays with the word in her head. She whispers it to herself to learn its texture, the way the sounds feel as they rise from her throat and pass through her lips. She comes to recognize the taste of this word. It is sharp and metallic, like the insides of her cheeks when chewed raw.

. . .

"WHO ARE YOU?" This is the first question the dibia asks on Adanna and her mother's third visit. The second visit had been easy, like swallowing a ball of fufu with okro soup. Adanna had arrived that day with her mother, feverish with fear. But the dibia had spoken to her the whole time like an uncle she would be fond of if only she got to know him better. He'd asked her about school and whether she fell sick often. He'd asked if she was scared of the dark. He'd wanted to know if she saw the same people, unknown to her in her real life, in her dreams, and if they ever invited her to strange places, like across a river or to a pit toilet. This time the questions hadn't come rushing out like water from a burst pipe, and Adanna had answered truthfully—no, she did not fall sick often; no, she did not swim across rivers or go to toilets in her sleep. Truthful except for the question about friends. She'd lied and said she had three instead of zero, because she didn't want to explain that her friends never stuck around after their parents met her mother, her face murky like storm clouds. Adanna had left that day clutching the sweets and biscuits the dibia had given her and wondering why she had found him so menacing before.

And so now Adanna is perplexed at the dibia's question.

"I am Adanna . . . Nwachukwu."

"Ehn. But *who* are you?"

Adanna looks at her mother.

"Don't look at me. Answer the question."

"I . . . I am a girl?"

"Where did you come from?"

"Number twelve Atilola Street."

The dibia is silent, waiting.

"Surulere," Adanna adds and, after a slight pause, "Lagos."

"Where did you come from?"

The dibia shouts the question this time, startling Adanna. Her eyelids flutter, and she struggles to hold in sudden tears.

Adanna hears her mother sigh. "Why is she crying now? Nobody touched her."

"Crocodile tears," the dibia says. "That's how they behave."

Adanna wants no part of this *they*. She should have known as soon as they arrived, as soon as she saw the dibia sitting unsmiling on his mat, his back straight as a cane, that this visit would not be like the last.

The dibia asks again, "Where did you come from?"

"Number twelve Ati—"

"Where is your real home?"

Adanna feels a headache start to bloom in her temples.

The dibia carries on. "Where is your iyi-uwa?"

Adanna looks to her mother again, but there is no comfort in the stony presence beside her. She asks the question that has plagued her for days. "What is iyi-uwa?"

The dibia peers into Adanna's face for a long time, and Adanna holds her breath. Finally, he lets out a bark of laughter. "She asks as if she doesn't know," he says. And then, with something like admiration, he adds, "This one is stubborn." He turns to Adanna's mother and speaks for a long time in Igbo. Adanna's mother nods over and over. Before they leave, more money vanishes into the dibia's robe.

They return home, and Adanna's mother whirls about the apartment, muttering to herself. She gathers all the food in the fridge into a large plastic bag and takes it out to throw away. She empties the kitchen cupboards of the nonperishable items, stuffing them into her section of the wardrobe among her clothes and shoes. She locks the wardrobe and tucks the key in her bra. Adanna follows her mother's movements, panic stirring in her belly, as their food vanishes. She tells herself there is a reason for this new strangeness and that somehow, even though she cannot see how, it will make sense. Maybe the dibia ordered her mother to get all new food because something in the air, a terror without a name, has infected everything they have. Maybe with their apartment purged of the old, her mother will go to market and all the things she brings back will be pure.

But her mother goes nowhere. At dinnertime, the kitchen stays cold. Her mother's body lies unmoving on the bed, the only light the glow from the TV. Adanna stares at her mother. In the near darkness, her face appears almost kind, and Adanna is emboldened to ask, "Mummy, are we not eating?"

Her mother sighs and rolls over, facing the wall. "We are fasting," she says.

Adanna sits before the TV, her insides aching. When she climbs into bed, she lies as far from her mother as she can manage. Still, the heat from her mother's body comes at her in waves, and she falls asleep to a sensation like burning.

. . .

BY THE SECOND MORNING OF THE FAST, Adanna has exhausted all her moves: the begging, the pacing from bedroom to kitchenette, opening the fridge to find it gleaming white and empty, its insides scrubbed clean of all spills and morsels of anything remotely edible. She is done with licking flakes of ice from the inside of the freezer; the water melts on her tongue and does nothing to fill the hollow in her stomach.

Adanna's mother keeps watch. They both stay locked in the small apartment, avoiding each other's bodies. Every once in a while, her mother asks, "Are you ready? Should I call the dibia?" and Adanna uses what feels like the last of her strength to say, again, that she does not know this iyi-uwa.

. . .

PALE BLUE WALLS GREET ADANNA as she wakes, a thousand drums pounding in her head. The mattress she's lying on feels thin, unfamiliar. She keeps her body still, willing the banging in her head to quiet. The last thing she remembers is walking toward the bathroom at home, following the sound of her mother's scrubbing brush, to tell her to go get the dibia, even though she'd had no idea what she would say when he arrived.

A face slowly comes into focus in her field of vision: a gray head, watery eyes set in a patchwork of wrinkled skin, flared nostrils that look just like hers.

"Ada'm."

Her grandfather's voice is whisper soft. His hand, when he takes hers, feels like harmattan. Adanna weaves her fingers between his bony ones. She isn't sure what her lips are doing, but she hopes they are smiling. She does not want him to worry.

"The doctor says you'll be okay."

He leans down, and his dry lips brush Adanna's forehead. She breathes in his camphor smell, and it takes her a few months back, to the last time she saw him, that day when he'd shown up just as the school bell had signaled the close of day. "Your mother is not well," he'd said. "She asked me to take you." Adanna had recognized a feeling of relief as the breath she hadn't realized she'd been holding—was always holding—rushed from her lungs. She'd asked no further questions and let him lead her to his car. In the weeks that followed, Adanna stayed with him and experienced a kind of happiness that felt free of charge, not like a borrowed thing she would have to return. Her grandfather became more than the familiar stranger who stopped by every few months and sat awkwardly with her and her mother, his aura always somewhat apologetic, asking her about school and leaving behind checks that her mother would pounce on as soon as the door shut behind him. He showed her photos of the father she had never met, and in those sepia-toned images—in that flared nose, that delicate manner that came through even in frozen motion—Adanna had found portions of herself that her mother would not account for, answers to questions she hadn't known how to form. When she asked to see wedding photos of her parents, her grandfather's eyes glazed over with pain. She apologized at once. "Mummy doesn't have any," she explained.

Her grandfather sighed. "Your parents weren't married when you . . . when you came. I was angry with them for so long." He spoke the words as though they were being wrenched from deep inside him. "You're the only family I have left, you know." A pause. "And your mother, of course."

The day before Adanna was to return home, she'd gone crying to her grandfather, begging him not to take her back. Her tears stopped only when they reached a compromise: he would ask if Adanna could visit with him more often, maybe spend school holidays at his house. When he dropped her off the next day, he asked to have a quick word with her mother, and they went to sit inside his car. Adanna watched the car with every shred of attention she could muster, as if she could see through the metal and tinted windows if she tried hard enough. Minutes later, the passenger's side door flew open and her mother stormed out of the vehicle, ignoring the old man hurrying out of the car, calling her name. Adanna, fighting hard not to cry, stood on the threshold of her mother's apartment, looking from her stooped grandfather standing defeated by his car to her mother's fast-approaching figure. When Adanna's mother got to the front door, she grabbed Adanna by the arm and shoved her inside, Adanna trying in vain to catch one last glimpse of her grandfather.

Now her grandfather straightens up, and Adanna sees that they are not alone in the hospital room. There is a man in a white coat, a stethoscope dangling from his neck, and her mother stands by the door. Adanna squeezes her grandfather's hand for comfort.

"We should let her rest," the doctor says. He leaves the room, and Adanna's mother and grandfather follow behind him. For a while, all is quiet. Then raised voices, her grandfather's anger coming through even as her mother tries to shout him down. Adanna cannot hear their words, but she makes them up in her head, imagines a version that she would like: her grandfather scolding her mother, and her mother taking it with a bowed head. But Adanna can tell reality from fantasy, and reality means her grandfather slowly growing silent, cowed, and Adanna returning home with her mother. Reality means at least a week of innuendos about wicked old men who pretend to be good and try to take children—whom they never wanted in the first place—from their poor mothers. "They said I was carrying a bastard child, now they want to take my bastard child from me. Over my dead body!"

Adanna is discharged the next day with multivitamin pills, cans of glucose-D, and a recommended meal plan handed to her mother. She wonders what her mother said to the doctor about why she was brought to the hospital, what lies or versions of the truth she might have told. At the hospital's front entrance, Adanna's grandfather tucks a few naira notes into her hand without looking at her. "Buy biscuits with it." To her mother he gives a bulging envelope. "Please, don't take a danfo, for Adanna's sake," he says. "There's more than enough for a taxi."

Adanna's mother takes the money, a defiant spark in her eyes. Adanna is not surprised when, after watching her grandfather drive away, her mother leads her to a bus stop and they board a danfo. Every screech and shudder of the bus sends jolts of pain to Adanna's head, but she bears it in silence.

They arrive at their apartment, and Adanna's mother turns the key in the lock and ushers Adanna into the warm darkness. Adanna's feet feel like they have been planted in buckets of wet cement, but she forces them to follow her mother inside. Her mother locks the door behind them and heads for the kitchenette.

"Put that money your grandfather gave you on the table," her mother calls out. Sounds pour from the kitchenette, lids clattering on and off pots, metal against metal.

Adanna stands in the middle of the room, her eyes adjusting to the low light. The sole window is closed, curtains drawn. The apartment smells like old cooking and her mother's lotions. Adanna cannot breathe. The yellow walls, stark, unadorned, begin to shift, closing in. The days stretch out before her. She is trapped in the apartment with her mother and her mother's love and fear and hardness and rivers of tears and her many faces, and there is no escape. Adanna's entire universe is before her now, her mother the sun around which everything revolves.

Adanna lunges for the front door. She grips the handle, turning and tugging, but the door does not budge. She feels downward for the keyhole and finds it empty. She stifles a scream and spins around to look for the key. She finds her mother instead, arms akimbo.

"What are you doing?"

"I want to go to Grandpa."

Her mother flinches. She stares at Adanna for a long time, but Adanna does not step away from the door. Her mother goes back into the kitchenette and returns with a plate of boiled yams and fish stew. She sets it on the table.

"You need to eat."

"I want to go to Grandpa."

Adanna's mother shuffles over to the bed and sits on it. She lowers her head and sobs, quietly at first, her shoulders trembling. Then she begins humming, the sound coming from deep in her stomach. Her back still against the door, Adanna slides to the floor as her mother's humming turns into singing. Adanna does not recognize the song, but the despair is old and familiar. She feels something breaking inside her.

Adanna crawls across the room. When she reaches her mother and attempts an embrace, her mother does not push her away.

· · ·

THE NEXT TIME ADANNA SEES the dibia, he is at their apartment. Her mother opens the front door and there he stands, straight and tall in his white robe.

"Your mother said you are ready to show us," he says to Adanna. "Where is it?"

Adanna decides to show the dibia all she owns and let him choose what this iyi-uwa is supposed to be. She goes to her section of the wardrobe and takes out a crucifix pendant.

Her mother is quick to react. "She is lying! I gave her that pendant."

Adanna rummages in the bottom of the wardrobe. Her next offering is the head of an old doll. The dibia frowns at Adanna and the head. "No."

Each time the dibia repeats the question "Where is your iyi-uwa?" Adanna procures yet another offering: the wheel of a toy truck long gone, a box of pebbles, an old headband.

When she has nothing more to offer, the dibia shakes his head like a father whose disappointment is eating his bones. "This girl is wasting our time."

After the dibia leaves, tucking his latest payment into his robe, Adanna's mother kneels before her. Adanna is so shocked by this gesture that she takes a step back, but her mother grasps her wrists and pulls her close.

"What have I done to you, ehn, Adanna? Why are you torturing me like this?"

"Mummy, please . . ."

"Tell us where it is!"

"I don't know what iyi-uwa means."

Adanna winces as her mother's grip tightens, searing her skin.

"Stop lying! The thing that you buried so you can go back to the spirit world when you die. You know what it is. You know where you buried it."

An idea begins to take shape in Adanna's mind. In her mother's Nollywood films, afflicted characters always return to their villages—the root of where they come from—when they need to unearth buried things. Adanna has never seen her father's village, and her memories of her mother's, from their last visit years ago for the burial of an obscure relative, are of red sand, the smell of firewood smoke, and not much else. But she is desperate for some relief from her mother's onslaught.

"It's in your village," she says.

Her mother's grip slackens, and her face loses its ferocity. She breathes out, forces Adanna into a hot embrace.

. . .

ADANNA, HER MOTHER, and the dibia arrive at the house in Umuduru late on a Sunday afternoon, after over nine hours in a cramped bus from Lagos. With Adanna's mother's parents long dead, the house is unoccupied except for the rare occasions when Adanna and her mother visit, or when her mother lets a needy relative stay there. Adanna takes in the quiet compound:

the small bungalow with a rusted roof and a veranda in front, old and dusty and in need of paint. Beside the bungalow stands a shed with a firewood pit for cooking and, at the far edge of the compound, a flimsy two-door structure made of mud and corrugated sheets, one side for the pit toilet and the other for bathing in. Adanna tries to think where she might bury a precious thing if she were a spirit child.

While the dibia sits on a low stool on the veranda, Adanna and her mother clean the inside of the house, uncovering squeaky old furniture and wiping off the residue from several harmattans. Then Adanna's mother hurries to the village market. She returns minutes later and proceeds to the backyard, where she cooks ofe nsala over firewood, Adanna handing her ingredients—stockfish, achi, utazi leaves—at her nods. Adanna watches the dibia eat. He does not look like a dibia in his T-shirt with sweat patches in the armpits and slightly too-long jeans, their hems brown with dirt. She wonders if he feels like a different man outside his white robe, if his vision is the same without the chalk circle around that one eye. She wonders how many more rolls of cash will pass from her mother to him.

Adanna is surprised to find that she and her mother are not anonymous here as they are in Lagos. Her mother's old friends and relatives pour into the small living room that evening, and even though Adanna does not recognize any of them, they call her by name, and she is unable to hide. They ask her questions in Igbo, and when she responds with wordless smiles, they wag fingers at her mother and make sly comments about parents who move away from home and neglect to teach their children their language.

They let Adanna sit with them, and they tell her how all the young men in Umuduru used to pursue her mother back in the day, how only after she left for Lagos did they begin to see that there were other women in the village. In the yellow light of hurricane lamps, Adanna watches her mother's face go soft and bashful, and for one brief, agonizing moment, she understands how someone might bring themselves to love her.

. . .

THE NEXT MORNING, the dibia wakes Adanna, asks her to point the way to her iyi-uwa. He is back in his white robe now, but Adanna is not afraid. She has seen him in jeans and a T-shirt, seen him lick her mother's soup off his fingers. She is not moved by the sharp edge in his voice. Still, she rises from her mat in the sitting room, where she slept, rinses her face in the backyard, and eats the breakfast her mother set out for her.

She steps outside the house to find the dibia, her mother, and two bare-chested men with shovels waiting for her. Anxiety rises in Adanna's stomach. Before they'd left for Umuduru, the dibia had warned Adanna and her mother to keep the purpose of their visit quiet, to ward off any possible interference from evil spirits disguised in human flesh—"With your mortal eyes, you can never tell who they are." To preserve the secret, the dibia had stayed hidden in the room her mother had prepared for him while the visitors from the previous evening lingered. Adanna had been thankful for the secrecy. But now, with this posse, she feels conspicuous. For a moment she wishes she were back in Lagos, where people only steal glances, never breaking their stride as they go about their lives.

The dibia nods, and Adanna begins to walk. She leaves her grandparents' compound, her mother, the dibia, and the men with shovels following. They walk down the road, passing houses with old people watching from verandas, chewing-sticks dangling from loose lips.

Adanna lets herself be soothed by the cool breeze and the smoky smell it carries. Dust rises from the unpaved road as she walks, and soon her feet are coated reddish brown. Adanna is not used to the quiet of the morning in this village, but she does not miss the roar of Lagos traffic or the sporadic episodes of road rage. She can hear the bare-chested men in conversation behind her, quiet, as though worried about breaking her concentration.

They arrive at a junction, and Adanna pauses. She listens behind her, hears the last footsteps stop, waiting. Waiting for her, she realizes with a burst of pleasure. After a mental coin toss, Adanna turns left, and four pairs of feet turn with her. As she walks on, her anxiety starts to wane. From time to time she stops in her tracks for no other reason than to hear the footsteps behind her fade into expectant silence. The sun rises higher in the sky, and Adanna takes her small procession through streets and footpaths, past children playing in the sand and women balancing tall buckets of water on their heads, past farms and fields and the local primary school.

When she pauses to rest in the shade of a giant tree, the dibia takes this as a sign and directs the men to dig. Adanna supposes it is as good a spot as any and does not stop them. She watches as the men sink into the growing hole, throwing shovelsful of soil that pile up around its mouth, and she cannot tell whether she wants them to find something. After the men have dug for almost half an hour, the dibia asks them to stop and refill the hole. He calls an end to the day's search. They begin the walk back home, and Adanna glances at her mother's face. The disappointment she finds there does not cause her steps to falter.

The next morning, Adanna wakes before her mother and the dibia. When she steps outside, she does not wait for the dibia to nod her into action. Exiting the compound, she takes the opposite direction from the day before. Everyone follows without question. The day's expedition ends with another fruitless dig at a crossroads where two footpaths intersect.

The days go by, and after each dig the dibia is less able to hide his annoyance. Adanna's mother becomes more silent, withdrawn. But Adanna does not care. With each dig, she relishes watching the holes form, widening as the minutes pass, the soil darkening as the men go deeper. Whenever the diggers do find things—a gnarled root, an old bone, a broken-off table leg—Adanna shakes her head at each one. She knows that the thing she seeks will never be unearthed from a hole in the ground, no matter how wide or dark or deep.

· · ·

ON THE FIFTH DAY, the men are digging near one of two streams in the village when they find a piece of coiled metal that looks like it fell off an old machine. The dibia does not hold the item in two hands and offer it to Adanna the way he has each previous time the men have dug up something. He peers at the piece of rusted metal, and just when Adanna expects him to look to her for confirmation, just as she prepares to shake her head no yet again, the dibia declares into the pulsing silence, "We have found it."

Adanna opens her mouth to protest. But she sees her mother fall to her knees, weeping like she has suddenly been forgiven a great debt. The dibia's unchalked eye stares into Adanna's, daring her to contradict him, to plunge her mother back into despair.

Adanna lowers her head, and the dibia leads the way back to the house, where he will burn the object and perform a ritual to unbind her from it, rooting her in the land of the living. She walks behind the procession, beset by a fierce and sudden feeling of bereavement.

. . .

ADANNA'S MOTHER IS DIFFERENT WHEN they return to Lagos. She wakes up cheerful and cooks meals and helps Adanna get ready for school and dreams out loud about getting a job. For the first few days, Adanna regards her mother with suspicion, waiting for her changing faces to return. When weeks pass and this doesn't happen, the knot in Adanna's stomach begins to unravel. Perhaps the thing they had unburied in Umuduru was real and had belonged to her mother all along. Perhaps all will be well now, as the dibia promised.

But one morning, Adanna wakes again to her mother's unmoving back, to a face hidden from the world.

"I can't get up today, Ada. Leave me, biko."

And so the months pass, and Adanna's memory of her time in the village starts to fade. Try as she might, she is unable to resurrect that feeling that had taken root in her chest as she went around Umuduru summoning holes from the ground with a single gesture. All she is left with is a constant feeling of falling, but without the comfort of knowing she will hit the ground.

. . .

EARLY ONE SUNDAY MORNING, a stone-faced mother wakes Adanna and announces they are going out. In the bathroom, Adanna stares into the bucket of water her mother has filled for her bath and tries not to think what strange possibilities lie ahead. Before the dibia, before the wailing prophetess, there were others: babalawos and diviners from Ibadan to Benin, tongues-speaking pastors armed with large Bibles and bottles of Goya olive oil. She cannot remember a time when her mother was not offering her up.

Adanna kneels on the cool tile and lowers her head until the tip of her nose touches the surface of the lukewarm water in the bucket. She takes in a breath and buries her face in the water. She stays still, expelling bubbles of air from her nose, listening to them gurgle up to the surface. She does not move as her chest begins to burn and the pulse in her temple beats wild and urgent. She clenches her fists and keeps her face submerged until her entire being dissolves into nothing but her need for air. When she knows she cannot last a second longer, she lifts her head out of the water, and the sheer joy and agony of that moment is all that exists.

When Adanna emerges from the bathroom, her mother gives her a cap that sits on her head like a cloud, and a square of white cloth, which holds the scent and stiffness of new fabric. The cloth unfolds into a large robe that reminds Adanna of the dibia. Adanna can guess now where they are going: the white-garment church a few streets away. She searches her mother's face, but it is as blank as the matching robe and cap she wears.

They head for the church, a large two-story building that Adanna passes on her walk to and from school. Some mornings she matches her steps to the clanging of the cymbals and tambourines accompanying the raised voices from inside. She imagines the church members dancing shoeless, spinning themselves into white clouds.

They arrive at the church and hear singing from within. A wall of incense smell hits Adanna as she and her mother step across the threshold. She looks around the smoky interior divided by a carpeted aisle, wooden pews on either side, figures in white robes just like hers. The church's altar is decorated in shades of white and gold and holds an elaborate candelabrum. High up on the wall behind the altar, above a golden crucifix, a single eye gazes down on the congregation.

Adanna settles into her place on the pew beside her mother and prepares to mimic the motions of the people around her. She bows when they bow, moves her lips when they murmur prayers, and chants hallelujahs when they do. Next to her, her mother moves her lips in time with the others', transfixed by the man in the elaborate purple-and-gold robe at the pulpit. Adanna wants to be back home in the bathroom, with a full bucket and her head down. Maybe next time she will breathe in a little bit of water, let it burn through her lungs.

After the service, Adanna's mother tugs at her hand, and they rush out of the main hall and down a corridor to join the end of a queue rapidly forming in front of a closed door. Her mother stretches her neck longingly toward the head of the line, muttering something about how they should have moved faster, there are so many people ahead of them.

"Mummy, church is over," Adanna says, and her mother turns to look at her with a frown that would have silenced her before. "Why are we waiting here?"

"We need to see the apostle," her mother says after a moment.

"Why?" Adanna feels her heart pounding in her chest, hears the tremor in her voice, but she keeps her gaze steady on her mother's face. "The dibia said everything is fine now."

Her mother's lips part, but there is no sound. A pleading, desperate look appears on her face before she turns away. Adanna knows now, as surely as she knows her mother's faces, that none of it—the wailing prophetess, the dibia, the person behind that door—is about her. Even as the thought forms in her mind, she feels like she has always known. Whatever happens with this apostle, there will be some other door to queue in front of, a new mountain to climb, a different buried thing to unearth. And her mother will be there, searching for something Adanna cannot give.

Adanna's mother squats so that their faces are level and squints at her with a fiery intensity. Adanna's breath comes quick and shallow. Finally, her mother will lay a confession before her, tell her something true.

"Ada'm, are you hungry?"

Adanna blinks like she is waking from sleep into a blinding light. Her mother's face is sincere, her eyes now clear and untroubled, and Adanna wonders if she only imagined the turmoil she'd seen just moments before. Her mother smiles, the lines around her mouth, the curves of her cheeks, the stretched lips, and the even, white teeth all conspiring to create the illusion that happiness is the only thing her mother's face was made for. Adanna wants to scream, *Liar, liar!* at the face and watch it crumble. But her throat is tight with tears now, and if she dares to make a sound, she will be the one to fall to her knees.

Her mother's voice is kind. She holds out her hand to Adanna. "Will you eat jollof rice?"

Adanna feels herself sinking. She looks around her at the long line of white-clad figures: angels or sinners, all of them, waiting at the door to heaven. But she knows that there is no salvation behind that door, just as she knows that no savior waits for her outside the church walls. Not her weak, gentle grandfather, with the sadness and guilt that bend his shoulders. Not the strangers far away in Umuduru. Not any dibias or apostles or gods.

Adanna nods yes and lets her mother take her hand. Their matching robes are the same white as plain boiled rice before it is stained red by tomatoes and peppers and betrayal. Adanna knows that when she swallows her mother's jollof rice, it will slide down her throat, warm and easy like an old lie. It will settle in the pit of her stomach like it belongs there.

Acknowledgments

THE STORIES IN THIS COLLECTION HAVE COME TOGETHER in the space of over a decade, and I have been privileged to have the support of so many.

I am immensely grateful to:

My agent, Renée Zuckerbrot. Thank you for believing in my work, for championing these stories, for molding them with me, and for being a trusted advocate and sounding board in sharing my work with the world. Thank you also to everyone at MMQ Literary Agency, and to Anne Horowitz for providing additional editorial expertise and guidance.

The editors at the following publications, in which the stories in this book appeared in earlier form: ZYZZYVA, *One Story*, *A Public Space*, *Ploughshares*, the *Kenyon Review*, *Lagos Noir*, *The Best American Nonrequired Reading 2019*, *Per Contra*, and *Ember*. Thank you for giving these stories their first homes.

The Tin House team, for embracing this book with more enthusiasm than I could have imagined, and for providing the perfect home for my first book. Thank you to Craig Popelars, Nanci McCloskey, Becky Kraemer, Jacqui Reiko Teruya, and Masie Cochran. Thank you to Beth Steidle for the stunning cover, to Meg Storey for the thoughtful copyediting, and to Lisa Dusenbery for proofreading. Thank you to Elizabeth

DeMeo, for the kind and insightful comments that helped these stories take their truest form. She is one of the most thoughtful, thorough, responsive, energetic, and conscientious editors I've worked with. She aims for perfection, and I have really enjoyed working with her.

Art Omi, Kimmel Harding Nelson Center for the Arts, Virginia Center for the Creative Arts, and the Anderson Center at Tower View, for providing space for me to immerse myself in the work. I also owe a debt of gratitude to Todd Hearon and the George Bennett Fellowship at Phillips Exeter Academy for providing me with a home to work and live during a tumultuous time. To Keenan Norris and the Martha Heasley Cox Center for Steinbeck Studies, thank you for the immense honor of a Steinbeck Fellowship; and to the Elizabeth George Foundation, thank you for the support and validation.

My writing teachers and cohorts at University of Manchester, Virginia Tech, and University of Nebraska-Lincoln. Thank you for reading early drafts of these stories, and for providing space for learning and growth. Thanks to Geoff Ryman, Ed Falco, Matthew Vollmer, Evan Lavender-Smith, Lucinda Roy, Timothy Schaffert, Joy Castro, and Jonis Agee for the support and recommendations that have helped open doors for me over the years. Thank you to Erika Meitner, for making my time at Virginia Tech gentler.

The Bread Loaf Writers' Conference and Tin House Summer Workshop, for the friends and connections made. Thank you to Lesley Nneka Arimah for the brilliant teaching that captivated me. And to my teachers and cohort at the 2011 Farafina Trust Creative Writing Workshop, thank you for first convincing me, all those years ago, that I am a writer.

My friends: Pemi Aguda, Usma Malik, David Barker, Tochi Eze, Yinka Elujoba, Tolu Talabi, and Dan Kennedy, for reading these stories at various stages, and for shared conversations and struggles. And to my UNL friends Zainab Omaki, Ber Anena, Tryphena Yeboah, April Bayer, Chaun and Tara Ballard, Kasey Peters, and Nicole Lachat, thanks for making Lincoln, Nebraska, feel something like home.

My family, for love and support, and my parents for filling my childhood years with the books that allowed my imagination to run wild.

UCHE OKONKWO's stories have been published in *A Public Space, One Story, the Kenyon Review, Ploughshares, The Best American Nonrequired Reading 2019*, and *Lagos Noir*, among others. A former Bernard O'Keefe Scholar at Bread Loaf Writers' Conference and resident at Art Omi, she is a recipient of the George Bennett Fellowship at Phillips Exeter Academy, a Steinbeck Fellowship, and an Elizabeth George Foundation grant. Okonkwo grew up in Lagos, Nigeria, and is currently pursuing a creative writing PhD at the University of Nebraska-Lincoln.